Firefly Electrics Series
Book 1:
Justice Machine
By Mark Furness

Liquorice Light Publishing

I0687789

Mark Furness is a bestselling author of thrillers and dark comedy crime. A former foreign correspondent in the US, the UK, Australia, and East Asia, Mark's stories often feature journalists, a prime example being the international conspiracy thriller, *Under Eden*.

Mark is Australian and based in Sydney. Join his Readers Club to free books by visiting his website. Find the link at the back of this book.

Justice Machine is Book 1 in the *Firefly Electrics Series* of crime thrillers with a comic-noir twist featuring electricians Lennie and Joe, and their sharp-tongued cockatoo, Rawcus.

Meet the electricians who re-wire Society.

● ● ● ●

FIREFLY ELECTRICS BOOKS:

#1 Justice Machine
#2 Kangaroo Court
#3 Galaxy Motel
#4 Gumleaf Mafia is coming soon.

About Justice Machine:

L ennie and Joe thank their lucky stars when they are fishing at dawn on a city wharf and a small fortune falls from the sky into their laps during a cargo-loading accident. They escape without being ID'd, and know exactly how to distribute the windfall. But have their stars been knocked out of alignment?

When Lennie's ex-parole officer, Trixi Talaveda, drops into their home for a chat about the missing cash, accompanied by the giant Enoka brothers, life becomes trickier than ever.

Will this new peril derail their plans to re-educate a man who persuaded Lennie's beloved Aunty Doreen that money really did "grow on trees" – and drove her to the grave?

Might a sea voyage with Aunty D's tormentor aboard their little yacht, *Flamingo Sky*, solve all their problems? Or might it all end in disaster?

In Justice Machine, as Lennie explains to their reluctant shipmate: "A machine isn't only a bunch of nuts and bolts...it's a word for a process that transforms things."

• • • •

*THE FIREFLY ELECTRICS books are written in UK/ Australian English.

1 – THE DAWNING

FOG sat upon the sea, speared by sunlight through holes in the clouds. On the deck of the small yacht *Flamingo Sky*, Joe peered into the mist through the telescopic sight of a rifle.

His companion cupped a hand behind an ear. "Sounds like an engine."

"We've got a problem," said Joe.

In the crosshairs of the magnified circle, the hazy, brown hulk of a ship was growing large. Filthy smoke spewed from its funnel.

"Let me see," said Lennie, taking the rifle and peering into the scope. "Jesus Christ! It's the *Lord!* She's gonna cut us in half!"

He tossed the rifle to Joe and pressed the ignition button on the inboard engine. It coughed with a nasty bronchial rattle and died.

Joe raised his eyebrows. "I told you to change those sparkplugs."

2 – PAPER RAIN

Ten Days Earlier...

JOE couldn't read far beyond street signs and his dead dad's Phantom comics. So Lennie read for him. It had started at primary school behind the scoreboard at the sports oval after classes.

Today, they were sitting under blue sky at a table in the back garden of their terrace house, a few blocks from their old seat of learning. They smiled at a white bird they'd named Rawcus who was standing on the table using his hooked beak and pink tongue to shuffle pumpkin seeds inside a bowl.

In recent weeks, Lennie and Joe had celebrated their thirty-third birthdays, a milestone that surprised them both given the journey. They liked their present age and had formed a consensus view that they would like their clocks to stop upon this number. As electricians, they knew the desired result could be achieved if they grabbed a live wire with their bare hands for long enough.

But they had people, and a feathered friend, who depended upon them, a nice house, a little yacht, and each other. So they figured that old age might eventually weary them as it did others. It depended largely, of course, on their future choices, the ripple effect of old choices, and luck.

And with regard to ripple effects and luck, there was a potentially nasty spanner that could fall into their works at any moment. So their eyes were peeled.

Joe glanced at the front page of a freshly printed newspaper that was on the table. He fought the urge to push it towards Lennie.

Joe wanted to know the contents of a particular article so that he could adjust the odds of him and Lennie being caught by any number of catchers for what they'd just done. Joe was the primary threat calculator in their relationship because he had a knack for assessing probability as opposed to possibility, the latter being more Lennie's turf.

Joe tugged an earlobe, opening the canal, hoping to let out a familiar noise. Lennie had said *anything is possible* so many times that it echoed inside his skull.

Right now, Joe wanted to get a grip on what was *likely* to happen next. Intense thinking about what *could* happen next, in Joe's experience, was a road to madness. Lennie had demonstrated that this road was a red hot laugh if occasionally travelled, like a day trip to a theme park, but it could be terribly disruptive to a person's life if it was continuous.

Lennie glanced at the newspaper's front page pointers to the inside stories. "Looks like we're on three," he said, comforted that their news sat upon an odd-numbered page. He trusted even numbers in the same way that he trusted some priests, accountants, teachers, parole officers, and policemen. Inside his head, he kept a file of the names and faces of key characters from these professions that he had encountered. The profile of an accountant was currently highlighted as *active*. The priest had been stamped as *completed*, but Lennie's attempts to fully erase this case note always failed.

Joe plugged a handmade cigarette between lips as plump as hot dogs, flicked a match, and lit up. He leaned back and felt the sun powering him like it did the new solar panels on their roof which energised the garden lights in the spare bedroom upstairs

Enjoy this moment, Joe told himself because if, according to the article, the news is good for us, the day just gets better. If it's bad? Well, why rush into that awareness on such a cracking morning? Although if the shit was about to hit the fan, it'd be handy to know when to duck. He looked at a timber paling fence behind a ramshackle rainbow of flowers in a garden bed beside the back gate. When the sun's shadow hits the pink zinnias, he'd call time on Lennie and get him to read the news.

Lennie sipped tea from a delicate china cup, put it back in its saucer, and resumed carving a slender stick of Bloodwood tree with a pocket knife. The stick reminded him of his Aunty Doreen, whom doctors had labelled a *Polydactyl* and paraded as a live exhibit at university medical schools years ago. As a kid, Lennie thought the name meant Aunty D was a type of dinosaur due to her crocodile skin. It turned out that they gave her the label because she was born with six fingers on her left hand, a fluke of Mother Nature that was the inspiration for the wooden carvings Lennie now called Lucky Jacks, or Jacks for short.

Wind swirled in the garden. Lennie slammed his fist on the newspaper to stop its pages from blowing away. There was frustration in his slam. Lennie believed in luck, and the regular practice of taking action to assist it, such as carrying a Jack in his pocket at all times, but he had stuffed up this area of operations yesterday. And he hadn't told the red-headed giant of a man who sat opposite him.

Joe curled his lips into an O-ring and blew smoke into the sky, careful to keep the chemical waste away from Rawcus who had the body of a torpedo-shaped football, a geometric similarity that some humans found it necessary to comment upon in the local pub from time to time. The latest occurrence was only days ago when

Rawcus had been walking casually along the bar sneering at other patrons and testing drinks that were not properly attended. It had not ended well for the commentator who, inspired by rum and a TV broadcast of a football game on a big screen, had attempted to grasp the animal, vowing to kick it to a mate. The bird's beak could guillotine bones, the would-be sportsman discovered. An ambulance was called. The police were summoned. Rawcus was cautioned, as were his two guardians.

Parading on the garden table with the swagger of a catwalk model, Rawcus showed off his tall, sulphur-coloured crest atop an axe-like head that was punctuated by blue-ringed black eyes, one of which he turned upon the bowl of pumpkin seeds. He used a claw to pick out a seed, then cast it aside in Joe's direction, sending it clattering to the pavement.

"Oh," said Joe. "We're Mr Fussy this morning, are we?"

"Shut up, bonehead," Rawcus shot back.

Joe shook his head. Rawcus was expert at parroting patrons from the Rose & Thistle where he had spent his formative years prowling the bars and beer garden, hanging from the ceiling lights – and listening. The bird had a terrifyingly good memory and, like his beak, was not afraid to use it.

Rawcus winked at Joe. He grabbed another seed, inspected it like a jeweller might a precious stone, and cracked it.

Joe shifted his gaze from Rawcus and peered across the table at a creature that looked so much like a black panther it made his skin crawl: although Lennie's head was clean-shaven and his skin the hue of honeycomb, it was Lennie's shape and how he moved that inspired this perception in Joe, aided by Lennie's fondness for wearing body-hugging black T-shirts and jeans.

Joe handed Lennie the reefer of a new strain of home-grown marijuana they were testing. Lennie sniffed the smoke wafting from its glowing nose.

"Mm," he said. "Hints of cinnamon and cocoa with notes of dark cherry and blackcurrent."

"You've been reading too many wine bottles," said Joe. "Smells like burnt skyrocket to me."

Lennie took a drag. He exhaled. "OK. Let's call it Mars Grass."

"You're the marketing genius," said Joe, who patted Rawcus's neck. Stuff the zinnia sundial, he thought. He nodded at the newspaper and said to Lennie, "Can we reboot that crystal ball?"

For 24 hours, Lennie had been scanning the news on TV, radio, and online – no alarm bells there. But the old-fashioned print version of the *City Daily* was promising its readers an *Exclusive* story about events that occurred on a wharf yesterday, including photos. The more he looked, the more the front page reminded Lennie of the lid of Pandora's box, which he had read about in a book on Greek mythology he once found in a prison library. When the box was opened, it released horrible curses. So Lennie puffed on the Mars Grass and admired the blue sky.

Joe tapped his fingers impatiently on the table. Rawcus turned a hard eye upon Lennie.

"Get – on with it!" screeched Rawcus. "You dozy fool!"

"OK, keep your feathers on," said Lennie, who rolled his eyes at the high-pitched imitation of a cook at the Rose & Thistle who'd been fired for workplace bullying. The workings of Rawcus's brain were a joyous mystery to Lennie; the bird's ability to blurt out remembered phrases was one thing, but knowing where to insert them for maximum effect took it to another dimension.

Lennie rested the reefer in a black and white ashtray that was shaped into the cuddling teardrops of Yin and Yang. He opened to page three and read aloud the headline: *Terror Money Rains from Heaven.*

The article described an "incident" that occurred yesterday at dawn. It had been an unremarkable Monday morning, drying out from a rain-washed Sunday night.

• • • •

THE ACTION BEGAN BREWING at a rust-eaten dock first hammered into Sydney Harbour a hundred years ago. Now the backwater was used mostly by foreign owners of small ships who were happy with B-grade facilities and C-grade security. The low level of investment by the State saved taxpayers money, and Lennie and Joe preferred that their taxes go to schools and hospitals.

They weren't too chuffed by rumours that the C-grade security enabled customs and border patrol officers to walk into the shadows and collect backpacks of cash and other valuables in exchange for blind silence about the full extent of the ship owners' entrepreneurial endeavours.

Lennie and Joe went to the wharf because of the fishing.

So carrying their rods, bait, and breakfast, they had stepped through a liftable flap in a chain wire mesh fence that was fastidiously maintained by locals.

Lennie, the founder and Chief Executive Officer of the Firefly Electrics Company, and Joe, his sole employee and the company's mental health manager, had enjoyed the early light sitting on the dock, their legs dangling over a wharf. They ate bacon and egg sandwiches, bananas, and shortbread finger biscuits which they had carried in a plastic bin bag. Lennie was a keen recycler and had folded and tucked the bag into a pocket of his hoodie, sensing it might prove useful again.

With full stomachs, they had turned to angling using bamboo rods, in part because of their old-fashioned look and the way they softly flexed upon both cast and reel-in, but the main reason they used them was because they were made of wood.

Wood, in their experience, had special powers, like water and lightning. It was composed by Mother Nature, like flesh and bone. Wood was their sort of stuff. So much so that Lennie made sure to touch a wooden little finger at least three times a day. These quick taps on his Lucky Jacks were low-cost insurance for their partnership against life's risks.

Lennie kept a range of Jacks in a wooden box on his bedroom dressing table like another man might collect fancy watches. The box was made from Bloodwood, a eucalyptus tree from which Australian Aboriginals extracted weeping red sap to treat, among other things, pain, which had both physical and spiritual dimensions that Lennie routinely grappled with. The container had briefly housed his Aunty Doreen's ashes – minus the soot of her left hand, which Aunty D had agreed to have amputated after her death but prior to her cremation.

In her last will and testament, she had donated the hand to a university medical school so they could examine it and then preserve it inside a block of see-through resin. Lennie had been minded to contest the will and claim the hand for himself, but Joe, who was working at the time in his role as Firefly Electrics' mental health manager, had suggested that wooden replicas of her extra pinky might solve a lot of problems. Lennie took the advice, although he often lay in bed at night plotting a burglary.

At the wharf around 5.30am, they had been dangling their lines, bare legs and feet, over the pier next to a rust-scabbed vessel named *Lord of Saigon*. The hoods of their sweaters were pulled over their heads against the morning chill.

The sewage pipe from the *Lord* had spewed a lumpy stew of unintended burley into the water. Lennie and Joe had dropped hooks into it, baited with white strips of octopus. A handful of plump pink snapper fish flapped about in their plastic catch bucket. Lennie looked up.

"Did God do that?" he had said, waving the tip of his rod back and forth at some peach-coloured streaks in the grey clouds above the horizon.

"Which God are you thinking of?" Joe said absently, regretting his bite on Lennie's hook as soon as the words left his lips.

"Delling," said Lennie, pleased at the question, his eyebrows lifting as if the answer was obvious.

Hooley Dooley, Joe thought, being careful not to say a further word for fear of sending Lennie off again with his Viking raving. Discovering his nanna's Norwegian roots last year had sent Lennie Larson blazing a trail through the internet to flesh out the origins of his life. Trust Lennie to end up among the gods and stars and get hooked on the idea that the Delling, the God of Dawn slept with Nótt, the Goddess of Night, who gave birth to Day.

Joe looked down the wharf at the *Lord of Saigon*. A four-wheeled crane on the tarmac beside the ship was going rhythmically about its business lifting bales from the long back tray of a parked truck.

Two men wearing green fluoro vests and yellow hard hats were standing on the tray of the truck, sharing duties to hook a chain from the nose of the crane onto the bales. The loads were then hoisted into the air, swung across the gunnels of the *Lord*, and lowered into its bowels. Lights blinked, bells beeped. Seagulls squawked angrily at the meanness of Lennie and Joe, who shooed them away from their bucket of fish.

"Hear that?" said Lennie, cupping a hand to an ear that had a chunk missing, trying create a better sound catcher.

"What?" said Joe, who tugged on his rod to draw the bait through the water and excite fish.

"Sirens."

"Miles away, mate. They're not coming for us."

"I've got a weird feeling."

"Beautiful spot, this," said Joe, trying to anchor Lennie's thoughts to the earth and sea. "We're blessed."

"You sound like Father Francesco," said Lennie, a bitter taste burning his tongue as he uttered the priest's name. Lennie pictured his six-year-old self in Father Francesco's car, prompting a Pavlovian response by his salivary glans. He spat the toxins into the harbour.

"Sorry," said Joe, looking down through the green water at thick flaps of waving brown kelp. He could have sworn that Father Francesco's face had just drifted behind the weeds, but he said nothing.

A terrible mechanical screech tore the air.

"Fuck me drunk," cried Lennie as a refrigerator-sized bale wrapped in black plastic tumbled from a snapped steel rope on the nose of the crane. The bale ended its fall with a thunderous thump and hiss of air. It burst and spewed rainbow-coloured contents into the air.

"Smuggled parrots?" said Joe, rubbing his eyes in disbelief.

"If they are, they need a doctor," Lennie replied, leaping to his feet.

Lennie grabbed a $100 note that floated past his face. He reached instinctively for the Jack inside the pocket of his shorts but failed to find it. His finger found a hole instead. The discovery of this non-existence made his spine tingle unpleasantly.

"Tie ya hoodie down, Joe," urged Lennie, tugging the drawstring tight on his own. He pulled the garbage bag from his hoodie pocket and shook it open. He smiled and said, "This is a gift from Delling."

"Sure," said Joe, lacing his hood.

They stuffed the flittering stuff into the bag, up their jumpers and T-shirts, down their underpants, and into their hastily emptied fish bucket. Lennie noticed a phone with a cracked screen on the tarmac; he tossed it into the bucket.

They squeezed through the flap in the mesh fence, trying not to get torn on jagged wire, and brushed past a faded sign that said: *This Wharf Is Under 24-Hour Video Surveillance.*

Lennie tried his pocket for the Jack again but it still wasn't there.

3 – TRIXIE TALAVEDA

I N THE BACK GARDEN, Lennie read out loud from the newspaper:

"Exclusive: A plot to secretly ship $30 million from Australia to fund an international network of Islamic State terrorists came unstuck yesterday when a crane driver dropped a bale of waste paper onto a Sydney wharf.

"The bale was filled with close to $1 million in cash, mostly Australian dollars but including Euros, British pounds, and US notes.

"A search of the remaining 29 bales at the wharf, some already loaded on the ship and others still on the delivery truck, revealed that each bale had been packed inside with used bank bills."

"Crikey," said Joe, rubbing the ruddy stubble on his chin. "That crane driver's slip-up has put a swerve on a lot of lives."

Lennie nodded and ploughed on:

"The bales, being loaded on a vessel named Lord of Saigon, *were described in the ship's log as waste newspaper destined for recycling in a factory near the Port of Iskenderun in southern Turkey, near the border with Syria.*

"A navigation chart on the vessel showed a route with stop-offs in Somalia, Yemen, Saudi Arabia, and Egypt. These are all countries where IS has active cells that have survived the devastation of the extremist group in Iraq and Syria.

"A government official, who did not want to be named, said Western intelligence agencies believed the money was destined to be dropped in batches to IS agents in these countries.

"The official said the money was believed to be the proceeds of an IS-related drug dealing syndicate.

"The Turkish paper factory was linked to a Russian military arms maker suspected of supplying weapons to IS in Syria – as well as the regime of Syrian dictator, Basher al-Assad, including banned chemical warfare agents that he has used on his citizens."

"Hang on," said Joe. "So these Ruskies are playing both sides of the fence?"

Lennie nodded. "That's the military-industrial complex for you the world over."

"Can I have that in plain English?"

Lennie huffed smoke. "Arms manufacturers like to make sure both sides in a war are equally tooled up."

"So it's a fairness thing, yeah?"

Lennie nodded. "Otherwise, the fight won't last past a couple of rounds."

"OK, I think I get it," said Joe. "If it's a first-round knockout, everyone wants their money back. But if the punch-up goes fifteen rounds, the promoters make a killing."

"Something like that," said Lennie, who was side-tracked by a whiff in the air: he could have sworn that Aunty D's lavender perfume was floating into his nostrils. But he was pretty sure the aromatic visitor would move on quickly, and without the addition of voices and the sensation of touch. Lennie didn't have time for doctors' claims that he suffered from a thing called *psychosis* from time to time – and therefore should not take perception-altering substances unless, of course, it was their medically-approved, industrially-manufactured gear called *anti-depressants* and the like. Still, despite this confidence in his mental faculties, Lennie, ever conscious of possibility, reached across the table and touched Joe's arm to make sure his friend's body was not an apparition. He returned to reading the news.

"OK, here's our bit."

"Police are searching for two fishermen who escaped with an estimated $500,000. Anyone with information should phone Crime Stoppers."

"Sneaky fuckers!" Joe blurted. "We only got a bit over two hundred!"

"Sneaky fuckers!" agreed Rawcus, a pumpkin seed slipping from his claw onto the table.

Lennie shook his head. "Coppers must have put their hands in the honey pot, and now they're trying to stick it on these *mystery fishermen.*"

Lennie showed Joe a series of grainy grey photos reproduced from the wharf's CCTV.

"Oh, shit," said Lennie. "That's terrible luck for the coppers."

Joe nodded. "That's what happens when you go cheap-arse on maintenance."

In the pictures, two blobby, dark figures shaped like Sumo wrestlers wearing hoodies lugged fishing rods, a bucket, and a bulging sack. Their faces were blurred like porridge.

"Lucky we didn't take handsome with us," said Lennie, eyeing Rawcus. "We'd have stood out like Long John Silver on that wharf."

Joe winked. "We could've cut off his crest and turned him into a seagull."

"Shut up, you boneheads!" screeched Rawcus, who'd stepped on the lip of his bowl and spilled seeds over the table. "Ah...see what you've done?"

Joe stepped to a hip-high steel drum from which smoke was rising. He stirred the flaming contents with a broom handle; red and orange tongues licked from the tip when he pulled it out. He surveyed the ashes. They'd burned their fishing clothes yesterday, but upon a second wave of analysis this morning, they had decided to burn every hoodie in the house.

"Our chances of capture?" said Joe, using the flames coming off the broom handle to light a fresh joint which he'd plucked from a bowl of pre-rolled Mars Grass on the table. "Mm...after seeing those pictures?" He tapped his forehead: "I calculate sweet FA."

Lennie wanted to agree with Joe about sweet fuck all, but Joe still didn't know the Jack had been missing from Lennie's pocket on the wharf.

Joe said, "No need to pull down the growing room, is there?"

Lennie looked up at the back wall of their terrace and the drawn blinds on the window of the spare bedroom upstairs. Lennie as an electrician, and Joe as a skilled gardener, could rig things such as solar-powered, hydroponic growing rooms with ease. Pulling it down might be wise, but it would have the consequence of inflaming the ire and suspicion of Trixie Talaveda. Plus there was another more pressing job they needed to keep on track that required a secret sea voyage in a few days.

"Business as usual, I reckon," said Lennie, taking the remains of the joint offered by Joe. "Do you want a bandage for that?"

Lennie gazed at a gash on Joe's right palm that had been opened while the big feller was stacking squares of rust-crusted steel building mesh against a fence by the back gate to the lane earlier. Joe's blood had stained the mesh which was destined for a seabed, and Lennie now wondered if a person's DNA could survive immersion in saltwater to the point of being detectable by police forensics. Was there a time limit, or a minimum quantity for such a chemical equation to be solvable?

"She'll be right," said Joe, who pressed his cut against the white singlet stretched over his freckled weightlifter's chest. He was more disturbed by a piercing burn on the side of his skull. Joe plunged the fingers of his un-cut hand into his knotted mop of red hair, digging a thumb into his scalp behind an ear to grind tangled muscle fibre. The tension always pinged in that spot, reminding him of his old headmaster's knuckles rapping on his skull. "Anybody home?" Mr Darian used to say, answering before Joe could reply, "No. Empty as outer space!"

Lennie cocked an ear. "Hear that?"

"Nup," said Joe.

"Listen up, knucklehead," said Rawcus, dispensing one of his favourite character assessments.

The wail of distant sirens wafted over the back fence. The chuff-chuff of a helicopter broke overhead. The trio looked up as the furious beast floated into view.

"Shit!" said Lennie, snatching off the table the bowl of joints and plunging it under his chair.

Rawcus shuffled close to Joe, who patted the bird's sulphur crest reassuringly, and grabbed the flapping newspaper with his spare hand.

The blue and white chopper hovered and tilted its nose down, dropping low enough for the ground dwellers to see the pilot's face, most of it hidden behind fly-eyed aviation glasses.

Autumn leaves on Joe's delicate Japanese maple were torn in the maelstrom. Squinting through the yellow and bronze confetti, Joe didn't need an English degree to recognize the word *Police* emblazoned on the fuselage. Lennie darted into the nearby garden shed.

"Faark," Joe hissed. Are the coppers smashing our front door in, he wondered, while we sit here like dopy ducks?

The chopper swung its scorpion tail, keeping its nose in one spot.

Inside Joe's skull, thoughts sprayed like sparks from a raging metal grinder. He grabbed a hot ember: it's never smart to run from a snarling dog; let's do a test before we draw a posse by acting guilty.

The chances of the pilot being a long-distance lip reader with the smarts of a bush turkey were pretty slim, Joe figured. But what the hell: he stood and pointed north with his index finger, mouthing into the mechanical din: "They went that way!"

The chopper swung away. Sirens howled louder.

The chopper boomeranged back.

The windstorm from the helicopter's blades ripped the newspaper from Joe's distracted grip. Pages flew, sucked up and tossed in all directions.

Lennie emerged from the shed, batting away floating sheets of newsprint. Rawcus's eyes were as wide as coat buttons.

Joe coaxed Rawcus onto his arm and called to Lennie, "Let's hit the tunnel!"

Joe moved towards the shed, heading for a trapdoor in the floor and a steel rung ladder built by Lennie's granddad that descended into the labyrinth of a forgotten coal mine that had fed boilers in steam-driven local factories a century ago. In the corner of his eye, Joe saw a dark object sailing over the back fence.

Thud! A black backpack slid to a halt on the brick paving in front of Lennie and Joe.

"This is weird," said Lennie. "First the wharf rains money on us, now this?"

Joe nodded at the motionless UFO. "Could be a setup by the bent cops. Should we toss it back?"

Lennie tapped the Jack he'd been carving.

The backpack was followed over the fence by a wild-eyed, shirtless young man who was stringy as sinew and pale as boiled pork atop his filthy blue jeans. He bounced to his feet and stared with black eyes at his involuntary hosts. Outside in the lane, voices shouted, sirens whooped. Blue and red lights bounced off a lamppost and reflected into the garden.

Two coppers, pointing pistols and wearing flack-jackets, rose as if on stilts behind the fence. They aimed at the kid's back.

Joe glanced at Lennie. "Horse patrol?"

A copper yelled at the kid, "Get on the ground! Face down!"

The kid kept his back to the cops and stood tall. His eyes flicked from Lennie's eyes to Joe's eyes, going like windscreen wipers with pink balls plugged on the tips. His eyes stopped.

Lennie sighed. He'd seen that look before: the kid wasn't too worried about being turned into Swiss Cheese by a hail of lead.

"Don't do it," Lennie said.

"Why the fuck not?" said the kid, his chest rising and falling.

"See that bird," said Lennie, nodding at Rawcus perched on Joe's arm. "He'll be traumatised for life if he watches you get minced in a blaze of madness."

Crash! The timber gate flew open. A copper clutching a battering ram charged into the garden; he gasped for breath.

"His heart's fucked!" cried Rawcus. "Me dad went the same way."

Lennie, looking through the busted gate, saw the nose of a parked police paddy wagon. The blue-shirted gunmen behind the fence must be standing on its roof.

In the garden, the purple-faced copper tossed the battering ram and drew a Taser from his utility belt. He yelled at the kid, "Drop, son – or you'll get fifty-thousand volts up your arse!"

Rawcus bobbed and screeched, "Up your arse! Up your arse!"

The kid grinned at the bird. He dropped to his knees, then went belly down on the paving. The cop with the Taser rushed in and fell with a knee on the kid's neck.

Lennie said coolly to the copper, who reminded Lennie of a pit bull terrier, "You don't want to end up in there, mate."

"Where?"

Lennie nodded at the front page of the *City Daily* that was flapping against a flower bed.

The copper harrumphed, lifted his knee and stood, keeping his Taser aimed at the kid. A colleague jumped off the roof of the paddy wagon and loped through the gate to handcuff the villain.

"Do you keep that bird in a cage?" the kid said to his hosts as he was hauled off the ground by his captors.

"We've taken the door off," said Lennie. "Gives him choices. Think about it, hey?"

The Taser cop sauntered over to the drum inside which the hoodies were smouldering and sniffed the fumes. "Who burns stuff in their garden these days?"

"Just getting rid of some rubbish, aren't we Joe?"

Joe nodded.

The copper looked at the squares of steel mesh that leaned against a fence. "What's that for?"

"Oh," said Lennie. "My mate here's a sculptor, aren't you Joe? It's still at the concept stage."

"What's the concept?"

"Top secret," said Lennie. "You know what artists are like."

"Wankers, most of 'em," said the copper.

Joe grinned. Rawcus slanted an ear at the copper.

"Your talking bird," said the copper. "Does he just copy, or can he do his own stuff?"

"Bit of both," said Lennie. "He's been on TV."

"Anything I'd know?"

"Bird seed ads. But he got the sack."

"Why's that?"

"Abusive language."

The copper snorted. "How long will he live?"

"His mum fell off the perch at eighty-three."

The copper wrote Lennie's and Joe's names in his notebook and headed for the smashed gateway exit. He looked down at a fallen newssheet and put his boot on the edge of the photo of the mystery fishermen from the wharf.

"Lucky pricks," said the copper. "Scooped up half a million bucks. I bet they think they won the bloody lottery."

"Do you reckon they'll get caught?" said Lennie.

"Probably. There's a special taskforce set up to investigate that whole shit fight. State police, Feds, anti-terrorism."

"Sounds formidable," said Lennie, who was buoyed by the information and recalled a proverb about an overabundance of chefs working on a dish. "Do you think they'll suffer from too-many-cocks syndrome?"

"What?"

A siren whooped. "Got to go," said the copper, who picked the kid's backpack off the pavement. "We might be back to get a witness statement. Sorry about the gate. If you want compo, come down to the station and fill in a report."

"No big deal," said Lennie. "We're happy to assist the State."

Joe looked at his feet and massaged his aching eyeballs. He wanted to say, "Shut the fuck up, Lennie, and get this plod off the premises".

"That's very citizenly of you," said the copper, who turned to leave.

"What did he do, that kid?" said Lennie.

"Junkie. Robbed a chemist. Grabbed some cash and a few boxes of opiates. Worth a fair bit on the black market, I'd say."

Lennie nodded. "Sooner that bag is locked up in the police station safe, the better, hey. Wouldn't want it getting lost along the way."

Joe stink-eyed Lennie to tone down the smartarse act.

The copper hawk-eyed Lennie. "Have I met you before? You look familiar."

"No officer. I think I just have one of those common faces."

The policeman turned and ground a boot on the fishermen's photos.

As the police wagon rumbled away, Joe said, "Will you ever learn not to pull a tiger by the tail?"

Lennie grinned. "Let's put the gate back."

"Why do you think that kid picked our joint?" said Joe.

Lennie pointed at the garden shed. Bruce, their neighbour's one-eyed, deaf, black cat was stretched out and purring on the sun-drenched roof. "We're a magnet for a certain type of character."

Joe nodded at the shed. "You're grandad's tunnel. Did you get that trapdoor open?"

"Are you kidding? The bloody things rusted tight as a priest's wallet."

Rawcus flapped from Joe's arm and flew onto the roof to join Bruce. Bruce meowed and Rawcus squawked as if they were chatting. They looked down upon the humans.

Rawcus slanted his head as if thinking. "Wankers!" he called out. "Most of 'em!"

• • • •

WITH THE GATE RESURRECTED, Joe stepped across the garden to inhale the calming sweet perfume of white jasmine vines that were blooming on the paling fences that squared him and Lennie and shaded them from nosy neighbours.

Lennie checked the time on his phone. "We're running behind schedule. Let's do that engineering test run now."

Joe checked that his cut hand had stopped bleeding and turned his attention to the inflictor of his wound: the set of six, window-sized squares of steel mesh leaning against the back fence, each one made from the pre-welded rods builders used to reinforce concrete floors.

He opened the flaps of a cardboard box that was sitting beside the mesh, reached in, and broke from their packets eight heavy-duty padlocks. He used the padlocks to join the corners of the squares.

Lennie stepped into the garden shed. He emerged carrying an iPad and sat back at the round table.

"Next to a pyramid," Lennie observed, looking up from flicking through pages on his e-reader, "my favourite shape is a cube. And yours will flat-pack. Fabulous work, cobber."

Joe was into ball shapes and circles. But round things weren't suited to this particular job. He smiled, shaking his head. Why didn't Lennie just say what the steel thing was? A cage!

Lennie turned back to reading an article on the internet about what happens when you mix household bleach and rubbing alcohol. It said the resulting gas can ruin your kidneys and liver. It can kill. It was called chloroform. Lennie already knew that. He was just checking the mixing ratios. He decided to run a test and stepped back into the shed, returning with a green plastic bottle of isopropyl alcohol, a blue plastic bottle of bleach, a measuring cup, and a glass into which he mixed a shot of the requisite chemicals. He took a sniff. "Whoa!"

The gas didn't knock him out, but closing his eyes drew a ghostly lump tumbling out of the night-time region in his skull. The face of his ex-parole officer, Trixie Talaveda, bumped around like a deflating party balloon, farting with a raspy voice. Trixie was a childless, single woman about five decades old who had described Lennie's and Joe's relationship as one of "dysfunctional co-dependency" that needed to be dismantled.

The term meant bugger all to Lennie and Joe, who simply regard themselves as two sides of the same coin – and had ignored her advice. But Trixie gate-crashed Lennie's mind from time to time as unpredictably as she knocked on their real front door.

"It's unhealthy to view the world through the eyes of another," Trixie said when she first visited their home and discovered that Lennie read aloud to his housemate. "It's dealing in second-hand reality," she had croaked, flicking cigarette ash into her unfinished cup of tea. "You boys need to let go of each other and see your separate ways."

In the garden, Lennie managed to burst Trixie's balloon by squeezing the Jack he had just carved. He forced his thoughts to turn left and reasoned, silently, that because the vast majority of the dodgy cash at the wharf was quickly recovered by the authorities, the main weight of the investigation by that special taskforce – at least officially – would be leaned against finding the source of the moolah and probing its links to IS and the Russian arms maker, rather than hunting two fishermen who had exploited a lucky break. But he knew people of some kind would come after their part of the windfall in time. He just didn't know who, how, or when.

"OK," said Lennie. "Now that we know your cube's a goer, let's hit the road to the cemetery, and plant some seeds of retribution along the way."

"Retri-what?" said Joe.

"We're gonna give those shifty shits from the wharf a taste of their own medicine."

Joe nodded. "Nice."

Lennie was determined that despite the countless possibilities he saw flying from their current situation, the normal rhythm of their lives must be maintained. Action must always trump contemplation, despite the pleasure he derived from the latter, especially over a few beers under a night sky while sailing their yacht, *Flamingo Sky*.

"I'll cut the flowers," said Joe, who noticed the tiny white petals of the jasmine vines on the fence were smiling at him with fairytale faces. Other beauties smiled at him too: beds of red and orange poppies, golden daisies, purple dianthus, and the tall-stemmed, pink zinnias. It's a miracle, Joe thought, that the cops and the backpack-kid didn't harm the flowers. But now Joe had to. He used a pair of large dressmaking scissors to cut the floral heads from their stems.

"Sorry. Good cause," he said to each plant as he went.

Joe tied the flowers in two bundles using purple and yellow gift-wrapping ribbons recycled from Rawcus's recent twenty-fifth birthday gift.

Joe had given Rawcus a mirror on his special day, so the bird could have company of a kind as he bobbed in his cage, which had its door removed in case Rawcus wanted to step out on the town. Sometimes Rawcus was gone over the back fence and into the sky for days on end to who knew where.

Joe knew for certain that some of the neighbourhood cats had a keen eye for Rawcus. The bird was good pals with their neighbour's cat, Bruce. But others wanted to turn him into dinner. Joe recently took to the vet a tabby moggy that had a white cockatoo feather in its mouth and a severed foot on the end of its furry leg. Joe took comfort that Rawcus also had the power of flight at his wingtips if needed in an emergency.

This morning, Rawcus stayed grounded and rode with the pomp of a Roman emperor on Joe's shoulder from the front door of the house into the street. They all climbed into a white work van. Red signwriting on both sides of the long vehicle read *Firefly Electrics*.

Lennie sat in the front passenger seat, placing the flowers beside him. Joe took the helm because he was a cooler driver than Lennie and almost never attracted the attention of the traffic police. Rawcus perched on a wooden rod fixed between the headrests of the front seats so that he could see out the windows. The van sailed away.

Rawcus swung backward headfirst, clinging to the rod with the elegance of a gymnast past his prime. The bird flapped back up in a blur of white feathers, unleashing a barrage of foul language. When Joe braked at a stop sign, Rawcus plunged forwards headfirst. Joe took every opportunity to send Rawcus into a spin. It kept the little feller fit.

The bird sidestepped the workout by hopping onto Joe's shoulder and clamping his beak on Joe's hair whenever gravity demanded, occasionally adding an earlobe to the mix, which had the side-effect of smoothing Joe's braking and acceleration to Rawcus's apparent satisfaction.

The trio cruised across the city, heading west to the Pinegrove Memorial Park at Blacktown Cemetery.

At a set of traffic lights, Joe was first in a line of vehicles waiting to cross the intersection. The signals turned from red to green. A lurking motorist accelerated from behind Joe into the inside lane and nearly clipped Joe's front bumper in desperation to get ahead of the Firefly. Joe didn't blink. Lennie wound down his window in fury.

"Fucking tool!" Lennie screamed, sticking his arm out and thrusting his middle finger at the offender's car.

"Try counting to nine, mate," advised Joe, knowing it was a waste of time suggesting even numbers like ten to Lennie.

Lennie counted to three for the sake of economy, and pulled his hand back into the van.

"Faarking tool!" Rawcus screeched, looking at Lennie.

Lennie scowled at Rawcus. "How about some original thought, mate?"

Rawcus raised his beak imperiously, as if such an idea was ridiculous, and turned to face the road ahead, tightening his claw-grip on Joe's shoulder.

Lennie looked at the flowers on the seat beside him. *Tools*, he thought. The dressmaking scissors that Joe had used to cut the flowers had belonged to Aunty D. She had taught Lennie that words were tools too, just like her scissors and the pliers with which he now cut electrical cables. He'd spent a lot of years collecting a kit of words and the ideas they made. He found reading as much fun as going to a hardware store, and he loved hardware stores. Bookshops, as far as Lennie could tell, were just hardware stores full of words. And how good were e-books, he thought? If he wanted to, he could carry a thousand novels in his pocket on his phone. How to use words was a trick though, the same as handling any tool. A string of words could be as dangerous as a chainsaw in the wrong hands. Their friend Pauline Gerrity, at her refuge for abused women and kids, was always stitching up those sorts of wounds.

Rawcus winked slowly at Lennie.

Lennie raised his eyebrows at the bird. "Don't you try that hypnotism shit on me," he said, watching his arm lift and extend outside the open window. His hand flattened and flew like a bird's wing, rising and falling. His thoughts flew too, backwards...he was in the beer garden of the Rose & Thistle Hotel, aged thirteen, sitting at a table drinking raspberry soda and snacking on potato chips, adrift inside the smog of one of Aunty D's cigarettes. Baby-faced Rawcus was standing on the table, chanting "three fives arr fif-teen...four fives arr twen-tee". Aunty D was clasping a glass of beer and leading the multiplication table chorus. She had drained her glass and turned to the newspaper's puzzle page to build Lennie's vocab using the crossword. Rawcus listened.

Joe slowed for another red light. Lennie's arm lost altitude, a tear dripped from an eye, and visions of the man who drove Aunty D to her grave piled into his head.

"Tick-tock," Lennie whispered, recalling the sheets of steel mesh that were leaning against the back fence at home, and the pile of padlocks beside them. "Tick-tock...Michael O'Hay."

Joe pulled up at an empty picnic ground car park on the Cook's River. Lennie extracted a mobile phone from the van's glove box and inserted a battery. He added a SIM card that he plucked from his jeans' fob pocket.

Rawcus busied himself in the back of the van, squawking in frustration as he clawed open drawers in a cabinet fixed to the wall, inside which Lennie and Joe kept electricians' things like fuses and plugs. One drawer contained crunchy pumpkin seeds. Joe regularly moved the seed drawer around to create a pick-a-box quiz to test Rawcus and keep his mind sharp. He didn't want him to become fat and lazy like some kept birds he knew.

"Where! Where!" yelled Rawcus, hurling drawers to the floor.

Lennie said to Joe, "Can you take cranky pants for a walk? I don't need his advice for this."

Joe plucked a few pumpkin seeds from his jeans pocket and popped them on his shoulder. Rawcus flapped aboard for a snack and stroll along the riverbank.

Lennie sat up straight to position his diaphragm for clear speaking.

"Hello, my dear," Lennie said to himself. "Hello, my dear," he said again, thinking for a moment that he knew how Rawcus's mind worked when the bird mimicked and repeated things. At its essence, Lennie saw the value of practice.

Lennie pulled a coin from his pocket. Heads would be the Australian Federal Police; tails would be the Australian Security Intelligence Organisation. He tossed the coin – and dialled the hotline number he had found earlier on the ASIO website.

"Do you have your recorder switched on, dear?" he said to the female voice on the other end of the line, although he was quite sure she had it on already. He'd read enough on the internet to know these things. And even though ASIO promised callers anonymity, she tried to get his name.

"Please. Just call me Mr Bird for the exercise," Lennie said.

"Now," he continued. "I was on a wharf in Sydney yesterday. You may have read about a cargo-loading accident and the discovery of hidden money. I wish to provide your organisation with some interesting names and phone numbers that came into my possession at the time."

The voice said: "Who do the names and numbers belong to, Mr Bird?"

"They are on a SIM card from a telephone that fell out of a bale of money and into my lap on the wharf, so to speak. I suspect, if you and your colleagues are nimble and quick, the SIM card and phone may lead you to a source of the cash and some shady characters with links to international terrorism."

"Well," said the voice. "It would be best if we could send someone to meet you in person."

"My name is Billy Bird, not Silly," said Lennie. "But if you can provide me with a post box number for your organisation, I will mail the objects in question to you forthwith."

Lennie jotted down the post box number on a scrap of paper and hung up. He dialled another phone number.

The male receptionist's voice said: "Welcome to the *City Daily*. Sam speaking. How can I help you?"

"Good morning, Samuel. Could I speak to Mr Thomas Steele, please?" Lennie sounded as toffy as a pinstriped English banker, or so he hoped. Seconds elapsed.

"Tom Steele," grunted the paper's Crime Editor and author of the article *Terror Money Rains from Heaven*.

"Listen, old chap," said Lennie. "I was at the Balmain wharf yesterday. I believe the long arm of the law is pulling your leg."

"How's that?" rasped Steele.

"Truth is, my colleague and I pocketed two hundred thousand dollars. Approximately. The Federales, therefore, must have trousered the other three hundred thousand. I believe the Police Minister is informed about this."

"Maybe you're full of shit," said the journalist.

"Get off your fat arse, Mr Steele, and do some work."

Lennie ended the call, enjoying the fact he was manipulating time in a way, turning it arse about. He phoned the office of the Police Minister via the Parliament House switchboard. But he was blocked, as he expected, at a desk inside the minister's office by a well-spoken receptionist who explained with joyful efficiency that the minister did not talk directly to random members of the public.

Lennie expected this because he had learned how politics works, in part, by watching political thrillers on the TV and watching the news. But he learned even more by frequenting pubs and bars around the city, places inside which he discovered that pollies, and coppers, and captains of industry, and journalists get drunk to gibbering, mainly from Mondays to Fridays of the so-called *working week*.

In these places, Lennie had drifted in the background, wearing an average business suit and a glum face, pretending to sip white wine, playing with his phone, and listening to the patrons brag and back-stab each other, especially when someone went to the bar to buy a round, or to the toilet to have a piss or snort a few lines. In fact, he got some of his best stuff by parking his bum inside a locked toilet cubicle holding a pencil and notebook with the voice recorder on his phone turned on. He had learned this technique for understanding the big end of town using advice from his aunty.

From her throne in the Rose & Thistle, Aunty D had been fond of saying to Lennie, "Go where the powerful go, just sit, say nothing, and flap your ears, love."

• • • •

"I UNDERSTAND COMPLETELY," Lennie said to the Police Minister's receptionist, "The Minister must, of course, stand aloof from the hoi polloi. The masses can produce a terrible odour and shed a range of bugs that may be deleterious to his health. However, I am equally sure your employer would not wish to grubby himself by involvement with things such as ill-gotten money, which is why I'm calling..."

"Are you implying the Minster is corrupt, Mr Bird?"

"Ha. I'm sure he makes do with his small but honest salary from the taxpayer. Though I have wondered what has afforded him that delightful waterfront home I've read about in the social pages that he shares with Mrs Goodbody. Have you ever been invited?"

"Can I take a message for you...*Mr Bird*?" the receptionist snapped. "We are very busy."

"Yes, please," said Lennie, picturing a fierce-eyed emu on the other end of the phone call. "As I said, would you like to record what I am saying? I'm recording my own copy, of course, via this smartphone of mine, just so there is no confusion later about what I've told you."

Lennie delivered the same message he had given to the Crime Editor about the missing three hundred thousand dollars. In speaking to the receptionist, he noted that he sounded like Rawcus again by way of repetition, but hopefully not by the timbre of his voice.

"Oh, that *is* very kind of you," said Lennie. "I do appreciate your concern about my mental health. But you should know that the media is aware I have informed the Minister's office of this discrepancy in his police force's accounting...what's that you say? Get to the point?"

Lennie stroked his chin. "OK, fair enough. In closing, I strongly suggest your internal affairs unit checks the CCTV pictures from the wharf with a hawk's eye – if they can find an organ of such optical integrity within their ranks. Failing that, the Minister might usefully arm himself with an unmarked, brown paper bag for the purpose of collecting samples, and drop into one of the boozers favoured by the officers who are investigating events on the wharf, and see who is the happiest and most generous at the bar...no, no, please...of course I'm not telling the Minister how to suck eggs. I'm sure he's most capable."

Beep-beep. The receptionist was gone. Lennie pulled the battery and SIM from his phone and dropped the handset into a brown paper bag that had previously housed a greasy fetta cheese and spinach roll.

He opened the van's door, stepped out, glanced around for onlookers – who were non-existent – and dropped the bag into a council bin. Best to dump the SIM in another location, he thought, just to be on the safest side of possible connectivity. The battery could be recycled. They had plenty more unused phones and fresh SIM cards in the locked drawer in the cabinet in the back of the van, a job lot purchased in Bali from their last sailing trip to the holiday isle.

Tools of the trade, Lennie called them, though he never listed such items on his annual tax returns for the Firefly Electrics Company. Lennie crouched and selected a flat stone from the gravel at his feet.

He threw it skipping into the river, losing count of the bounces before it sank. He sensed a presence at his back, but not one that made his skin crawl.

"Seven," said Joe.

Lennie had no doubt there had been seven skips. Because Joe had a proven skill for counting things at a glance, as he did with marbles in the schoolyard when they first met, and like he did later with darts scores in the pub. The pub darts champ, Bobby 'Bullseye' Donovan, reckoned Joe might have something called autism. As well as helping Joe count without thinking, it was a brain function that made him do things, now and then, also without thinking. Bullseye had called it "spontaneity" and said it was a quality to be treasured in a person. Lennie agreed with Bullseye. It was spontaneity, after all, that had sealed his and Joe's friendship at school through a legendary act that had since been erased from the school's official history. This morning, looking at the river flowing past like some cliché about time, Lennie recalled how their headmaster, Mr Darian, had labelled it an act of "blind stupidity" by Joe.

They climbed into the Firefly and Joe steered them sedately from the car park, reaching for the volume dial on the CD player to crank up ABBA's *Mamma Mia*. The boys joined in, though all Rawcus could utter was "Giss a kiss, love" repeatedly, loudly, and completely out of sync with every other sound. Rawcus had no sense of melody.

Minutes later, they stopped in a loading zone, near but not directly outside a post office.

"Got any cash?" said Lennie.

"There's two hundred grand at home."

"I'm serious. A credit card will leave a trail."

"By buying an envelope?" said Joe, unenthusiastically plucking a golden fifty-dollar note from his jeans' pocket.

Lennie thought that he needed to read to Joe the novel *1984* by George Orwell, or some more news stories about the Chinese Communist Party or Russian politics. He stepped into the post office and purchased a bubble wrap bag. On the way out of the PO, he dropped the change into a guitar-plucking busker's upturned cowboy hat and climbed into the van.

Joe said, "Generous."

Lennie shook his head. "If you'd copped an earful of that kid's voice, you'd have given him more."

Joe nodded. "That good, hey?"

"Imagine a hacksaw cutting a brick."

Lennie, who was naturally left-handed, scratched in black pen on the cover of the envelope with his right hand, listing the postage-paid-by-receiver, PO box address for ASIO he'd been given. He took from the van's glovebox the phone he had found on the wharf in the wake of a fleeing crew member of the *Lord of Saigon*. He slid the information-rich handset, which had a few banknotes wrapped around it with an elastic band to reinforce its authenticity, and its loose SIM card, into the envelope. They drove on a few suburbs and parked a hundred metres short of a street-side, red post box.

Joe donned a baseball cap and sunglasses, wandered up to the box and popped the envelope in the slot. Back in the van, he accelerated away to the sound of *Fernando*. Rawcus had found the drawer with the pumpkin seeds and on the floor in the back of the van, he snacked as triumphantly as a quiz show champ, stumbling now and then on the turns, complaining loudly about Joe's driving.

When they arrived at the Blacktown Cemetery gates, the van fell silent.

Joe parked in a bitumen lot. Rawcus was appointed watchman to stay in the van, where he energetically patrolled his rod, looking through the windows for any movements worthy of alarm.

Standing outside, Joe checked his reflection in a side mirror and combed his hair with his fingers. It was largely a failure because of so many knots. But he liked his knots. He recalled how headmaster Darian used to rake his hair knot-free with a greasy plastic comb when he was called to the big man's office after school and ordered to "shut the door, son."

Stopping at the cemetery gate, Joe straightened the collar of his checked flannel shirt that hung loose outside his blue jeans; he cleaned the toes of his lace-up training shoes by rubbing them over his calves.

Lennie patted his freshly shaven pate, licked a finger and ran it over his eyebrows to smooth them. He hand brushed a new black T-shirt and slim-fit jeans. His elastic-sided black boots were polished to a mirror shine. He'd left his sunglasses in the van to remove barriers between him and the two people they were about to visit. When communication really mattered, he believed in doing it with "naked eyes".

The Mars Grass was top-notch, and they'd last smoked it only an hour or so ago, but its grip on the synapses of the duo dissolved like fairy floss in the mouths of great spirits.

They laid the first bunch of flowers at the foot of the memorial for a nurse named Jacinta Turner. They'd been at primary school when she died. Lennie and Joe had never met her, but they had met most of her killers. The Colby brothers once lived a few doors from Lennie's nanna's terrace house when the old lady was alive. Lennie and Joe now lived in nanna's house, and the dark energy of the Colbys still fizzed from time to time through the rooftops and walls that connected many of the homes in the street. At least that was how Lennie felt.

The Colby-led gang had ripped Jacinta, whom they'd never seen before, off a dark street outside a railway station and terrorised her in their car for hours, bashing her senseless and raping her. When they'd had enough, they took her to a paddock where Bob Peters slit her throat with a knife and kept cutting, almost severing her head, while the others egged him on. A top night out that got out of hand, they told the judge and jury at their trial.

Jacinta's ordeal had crystallised a pyramid of ideas that Lennie called *Moral Principles*. The base was: *Do unto others as you would have them do unto you.* The second tier was borrowed from a line in one of Joe's Phantom comics: *Phantom is only rough with roughnecks.* This translated as: *Bad people should get a dose of their own medicine.* The crowning principle, based on Lennie's and Joe's religious experiences, was: *Make sure people reap what they sow – in this life.*

Over time these principles had morphed into their *ethos*, which Lennie argued was more palatable for public consumption. They printed this ethos on the backs of their business cards, and on their website. Joe believed it lost them some business, but Lennie countered that if people objected to their ethos they were arseholes and he'd never have worked for them anyway.

The ethos said:

Safeguard and have faith in Mother Nature.
Protect the innocent and vulnerable – people and animals.
Be cynical about the Establishment.
Be suspicious of all organised Religions.
Explore alternative perceptions.
Seek laughter every day.
Never abandon the ship of friendship.

Lennie and Joe had detailed plans for the Colbys and Bob Peters if they ever walked from prison.

These plans were developed over their kitchen table in discussions that spawned what they codenamed the *Ethics* projects.

"Soon, sweetheart," said Lennie as he placed the remaining bunch of flowers on Aunty D's grave. Their current *Ethics* project was accelerating. Just a few more days of preparation before they put the foot down on execution.

• • • •

WEDNESDAY MORNING.

Lennie walked to the local shops to pick up his only business suit from the dry cleaners. He believed he wore the navy pinstripe, with a white shirt and red silk tie, as well as any corporate titan, if you turned a blind eye to a missing incisor tooth and an ear that had a chunk missing.

After collecting his suit, Lennie visited the optometrist's shop next door, where he tried on a pair of black-plastic framed reading glasses which he picked out from a revolving stand.

The optometrist approached, breaking into a smile as sincere as that of a frog to a fly.

"They look great on you, sir. But the lenses are non-optical," the eye-man explained. "They are for display only. You know...for the look. We should test your eyes first."

"For the look only, hey," said Lennie, ruminating on the man's advice. "Mind if I wear them now?"

The optometrist smirked as he counted Lennie's cash.

Lennie smiled at the recurring realisation that life, at times, was an inescapable chain of contradictions, a clichéd maze of smoke and mirrors, a journey upon which it was easy to get lost. That's why the *ethos* was so important to him and Joe and Rawcus.

• • • •

FRIDAY EVENING. RAWCUS was having a night out, hanging upside down with some friends in the branches of a towering gumtree up the lane.

"We're a pathetic species," said Lennie as he unpegged a clean white shirt from the clothesline and looked at the feathered party-goers in the distant tree.

"How's that?" said Joe, who was watering a batch of fresh seedlings in a garden bed.

"Rawcus. Listen to him. Speaking cockatoo like a native, happy as. Then he can nip down the pub with us and crack the bar into fits with a few lines. He clearly talks another lingo to Bruce the cat. That's three languages. Most humans can barely master one."

"Want me to iron that?" said Joe.

"Thanks. I better have a shower."

• • • •

LENNIE DRESSED IN HIS suit, tie, and new reading glasses, and Joe drove him in the Firefly to a pub in North Sydney that was popular with office workers winding down from their terribly stressful weeks, as they liked to inform anyone within earshot. Lennie had been frequenting the pub on consecutive Friday nights. As far as Lennie could tell, they mostly spent the five-day stretches growing their bums and bellies. He adjusted his glasses as he stepped inside the Green Door Hotel.

The thick-framed eyewear was a new touch suggested by Joe, who reckoned they made him look as scary as a butterfly in a spring meadow. He reckoned the normal Lennie affected some people like a wild wasp trapped in a small room.

After dropping Lennie outside the hotel, Joe motored to a back street near a sports oval, where he parked and climbed into the rear to watch a DVD of *Toy Story* on a laptop. He had a folding chair to sit in, cold beers in a portable cooler, and a specially wired microwave oven to reheat last night's left-over takeaway of beef vindaloo and saffron rice. He put his phone beside him on a shelf to wait for Lennie's call.

In the pub, Lennie stood at the roaring bar and bought a beer at a price that almost made his blood boil. He waited for his prey. He bought a second beer. The wiry man with the handlebar moustache did not disappoint.

Michael O'Hay was generous to his staff at his office's regular *Thank God It's Friday* drinks. O'Hay was mostly a moderate drinker, Lennie observed, befitting his status as the boss and his responsibilities as a married father of two teenage daughters.

"I've had enough. I've got to drive," Lennie heard O'Hay say as he generously filled his mostly female employees' glasses to overflowing with the cheapest house wines. O'Hay was particularly kind to one of the youngest and prettiest girls. Lennie had not seen her before and guessed she was a new recruit to O'Hay's accounting firm.

Over previous Friday nights, Lennie had discovered that O'Hay, in a fatherly way, would offer to chauffer home the most intoxicated girls. They shouldn't be left vulnerable, he said to his colleagues. He sometimes took two girls at a time, dropping off one, and then the other, from his smart red Alfa Romeo coupé.

Tonight, after about two hours, O'Hay said his goodbyes and departed the hotel with the new girl tottering and leaning on his arm. He held his head like a proud father leading a bride to the altar, so Lennie thought, although Lennie had only seen weddings in movies and on the TV.

Lennie phoned Joe as he followed the pair into the street. The couple headed toward the pedestrian entrance of an underground car park.

As O'Hay's coupé nosed its way into the street, Lennie and Joe were waiting with their engine running in a loading zone near the car park exit.

They guessed right about O'Hay's destination. It had become a routine. Minutes later, he slid under the wide, leafy branches of a gnarly camphor laurel tree on the edge of a public park and stopped, turning off his headlights.

Joe cruised the Firefly past the Alfa, killed his own headlamps and did a U-turn, parking kerbside in shadow, a couple of stones' throws from O'Hay.

At the hotel earlier, Lennie had witnessed evidence that O'Hay had thoughtfully softened his planned experience for the girl by administering a powder of some sort to her wine glass as they moved past the opening rounds of drinks.

"She's probably out like a light in there," he said to Joe. "Or on her way."

Joe flashed a thumbs-up at Lennie, who nodded, putting instinctive faith in his friend's ability to deliver a surgical response to the tricky situation that confronted them, for they did not want to reveal their full hand to O'Hay this night.

Joe put on a black wool beanie, making sure to tuck all his red hair inside it, and donned a pair of wraparound sunglasses. He got out of the van, turned his jacket collar up, and walked to the driver's side window of O'Hay's car, which he rapped with a significant knuckle. Three times.

O'Hay refused to open the window, as Joe expected – though he would really have preferred the window open. After consuming four cans of beer with the curry while watching *Toy Story*, Joe has developed a substantial reservoir of recycled lager. He let it rain over O'Hay's window. The accountant's jaw-dropped mouth reminded Joe of a carnival clown that swallowed ping-pong balls. Too bad that window was closed, he thought. He waved an index finger at the cowering clown and mimed the words, *naughty-naughty*. The moustachioed molester kicked his engine into life and accelerated into the street.

Joe quick-stepped back to the Firefly.

Lennie said, "I reckon he's lost the taste for tonight, but let's follow the little turd to make sure."

They turned a corner and headed to the main road.

O'Hay stopped at a red light. His passenger door flew open, and the girl tumbled out. She flagged a passing taxi and jumped in.

O N THEIR way home, Joe parked the Firefly next to a small modern block of apartments in a side street close to their own home, where once-crumbling workers' cottages were now dressed-up with multi-million-dollar makeovers. The block had been the site of an old corner shop.

The shop in its heyday had a kitchen out the back which housed a wood-burner oven where Lennie's favourite strawberry-jam sponge cakes were baked.

Now, a few lights glowed inside the apartments. A TV screen as big as a double bed flickered on a wall in one of them. Lennie plucked two cans of beer from the drink cooler between the seats and passed one to Joe. They sipped in silence.

Before her death, Aunty D had sold from that shop, among other things, ham and cheese sandwiches made from white bread; ice cream scooped from stainless-steel tubs into sweet biscuit cones; newspapers; fizzy drinks; cans of baked beans; and laundry soap. She handmade lolly mixes in white paper bags for the school kids and sold them from a "Lucky Dip" jar. That was until mothers and fathers – who as children had put their own small hands into similar jars – saw a new light and insisted on hand-cut fresh fruit after school for their precious self-reflections. It was around that time that Aunty D realised that she and her shop didn't understand the world anymore. But her accountant Michael O'Hay did.

Under O'Hay's advice, a *For Sale* sign went up on the shop to assist Aunty D's "comfortable retirement" as O'Hay put it. He also kindly offered to advise her on how best to invest the profits from the sale: she should buy what he called *money trees*. And he could get them for her.

Aunty D was in luck on another front too. O'Hay had a mate who was a real estate agent who would value the property at a reduced fee. Sadly, the agent said later, the shop had rising and falling damp in its hundred-year-old brick walls, the timber floors were rotten, and it was cockroach infested. The shop came with an empty block of land next door that Aunty D used for storage in a tin-clad shed and for a clothesline, but unfortunately, that site was covered in thick concrete that would cost a small fortune to dig up.

O'Hay saved the day when another mate of his offered to buy the dilapidated shop building and concrete wasteland for a good price without the need to put it on the market. Advertising costs and real estate agents fees wasted so much money, O'Hay explained patiently to Aunty D.

O'Hay, at first, didn't say how much of his own blood, sweat, and tears he put into setting up the arrangements. He was a man who just wanted to "do the right thing" by a loyal, long-time client and friend in Aunty D.

Lennie and Joe had been sailing *Flamingo Sky* in another part of the world during the months when O'Hay helped Aunty D.

• • • •

NOW, LENNIE AND JOE looked through the Firefly's windscreen at an illuminated *For Sale* sign erected on the site of Aunty D's old shop.

Unit 5, one of nine apartments in the *Belle Vista - Luxury Residences* complex, was owned by Michael O'Hay.

"What's the asking price?" said Joe.

Lennie looked up the real estate agent's website on his iPad. He showed Joe the number: $1.5 million.

Joe said, "What do you reckon the whole thing's worth?"

"Well," said Lennie, "Based on the asking price for number five, which is one of the smaller apartments, and with four penthouses capturing views of the whole city skyline, I reckon the entire show is worth about fifteen million dollars."

"Cost to build?" said Joe. "Four to five million tops? Yeah?"

"That'd be ballpark."

"So O'Hay and his mates have pulled a neat ten million profit."

"Oh, don't forget the $395,000 they paid Aunty D for the site," said Lennie.

"Oh, no," said Joe, draining his can and flicking it clattering into the back of the van. "Let's not forget that."

• • • •

A WEEK LATER. FRIDAY afternoon.

Lennie was sitting at the kitchen table staring at the blank page of an A4 spiral-bound notebook, holding the nose of a fresh lead pencil in front of the hole of a metal sharpener. He recalled what Father Francesco used to say as he ruffled Lennie's hair at Sunday school, "You don't mind if I put my pencil in your sharpener, do you, Leonard?"

Lennie stuffed the pencil in the hole and twisted, watching the blade cut and the shavings coil. He'd hated pencils as a kid. Now he wouldn't use any other writing tool. He liked the way graphite reflected the writer's mood through shifting amounts of pressure and changing angles of attack on the page. Most of all, he liked the cutting of the wood.

He wrote *Ethics – Project 3* on the top of the page.

He began with a flow chart, starting at the Green Door Hotel in North Sydney and ending at a spot in the Pacific Ocean.

On the next page, he wrote a checklist of equipment which included a platinum blond party wig; a cocktail of household bleach and rubbing alcohol; plastic zip-lock ties; an air-powered speargun he had named *Mr Lovecraft*; and a packet of pelletised ammonium-nitrate explosive.

"Thomo," said Lennie. "So he didn't ask any questions."

"Nup," said Joe. "I told him we wanted the ammo-nitrate to blow up a rats' nest." .

Lennie smiled. Thomo was a tree farmer who used explosives to blow out stumps. He met the Ethos test because he was replanting his land with native species. The pellets had cost two kilograms of Mars Grass and, importantly, generated no receipt.

Lennie used his iPad and the internet to run a final check on the weather patterns and coastal tides. He liked what he saw: clear night skies, low swells, and light wind for a few days yet. He touched the Jack in his pocket.

"We're on," Lennie called through the kitchen door into the lounge room.

"Aye, aye, captain," said Joe, who was lying on the generous sofa in front of the TV.

Lennie checked the time. "We need to leave in one hour."

"Perfect," said Joe, popping the top on a can of beer. He was watching on the TV a pre-recorded rugby league match between the Eels and the Rabbits. The Rabbits were Joe's team. He hated eels.

Joe never watched a football game on TV unless he knew the Rabbits had won. Armed with this knowledge, with this rare piece of certainty in his life, he watched the same game over and over again, using the remote control to pause now and then on the faces of the supporters of the losing team.

Joe called to Lennie, "Those Eels fans don't know what's comin'. I can see the hope in their eyes, and I know it's useless. Must be what it feels like to be a God, hey?"

"I reckon," agreed Lennie. He began strapping an industrial respirator to his face to stop himself from breathing the fumes that soon smoked from the bleach and alcohol he was mixing in a large bottle in the kitchen sink. The formula worked best fresh.

But the respirator was faulty and Lennie caught a whiff of the chloroform. The room swam around him and he glanced into the lounge at Joe, trying to focus on a distant object to regain balance. The big redhead's hair made for interesting viewing: Lennie could almost swear Joe's skull was now matted with writhing, pink and purple snakes.

Joe lifted his head off the sofa's armrest and looked through the doorway at Lennie. "You right, mate?"

"I tell you what," said Lennie, pulling the respirator off his face and trying to ignore the snakes, which now looked like the gelatine lolly variety. "This stuff packs a punch."

"Good," said Joe, who turned back to the TV, plonking bare feet as big as diver's flippers back on the armrests.

Those feet, thought Lennie. They're bare now most days, and they were bare when we met them at school. Joe didn't own a pair of school shoes, or maybe they were always getting repaired. Lennie couldn't remember exactly. But he did remember the day this burly kid, wearing a short-sleeved checked shirt, which had a torn breast pocket, tucked into a pair of black football shorts, had literally rocked the playground. In class, Joe was always placed at the back of the room and handed pencils and colouring-in books. The teacher had given up on teaching Joe, who had no textbooks and, in fact, few possessions of any kind. But he did have ten fine marbles, or "doogs" as the kids called them, which he carried in a long grey sock. Until something happened.

• • • •

JOE'S MARBLES WERE called *Cat's Eyes*. They were beautiful balls of glass – balls being his favourite shapes from an early age – decorated with rainbow-coloured swirls.

One of the teachers' pets, Bobby Simpson, should have quietly pocketed Joe's doogs and walked away after he won the three games they played inside a ring scratched out with a stick in a flat patch of dirt under the keen gaze of a mob of other ten-year-old boys, including Lennie.

"Lost ya marbles, Clarkey?" taunted Simpson in front of the other kids as he dropped the glistening spheres into a royal blue, velvet bag that his mother had sewn for him and embroidered with the gold initials, *BS*. Simpson made sure to clack them loudly one by one as they fell in.

Joseph "Joe" Clarke should have been institutionalised for his reaction to the clacking, the headmaster, Mr Darian, said later to Joe while he was typing the incident report for the school authorities.

No thought went into it, Joe explained to Mr Darian. He simply wandered over to a garden bed, picked up a fist-sized rock, and stuffed it inside his now empty long sock. Then he added another rock because he liked pairs of things, and he wanted to hear his own "clack" as the two rocks hit each other.

Joe had gripped the open end of the sock and started swinging it in circles, forcing the rocks deeper and deeper into the toe-end.

He soon had his whole right arm roaring around. Joe said he wanted to fly himself into the clouds. But Joe knew nothing of the physics of aviation and propeller blades. He lost grip of the sock, or so he said, which soared towards the heavens.

"Dead pigeon!" cried Joe, as the missile began to fall. The other kids scattered.

Bobby Simpson was the school's head prefect and cricket captain, a handy batsman who had good eyes and quick reflexes. But he was busy pulling the drawstring on his bloated sack of marbles when Joe launched the sock. At Joe's pigeon cry, Simpson looked up in puzzlement at the unidentified flying object, which crashed into his gawping mouth.

"Shoulda kept your eye on the play, Simmo," said Joe, as Simpson spat teeth chips and blood into the dirt. A couple of years later, Simpson's fancy new front teeth popped out of his mouth after Joe bumped him during a football match. Lennie and Joe informed the other kids that they'd seen similar pink-and-white creatures resting in glasses of water at night next to Aunty D's bed.

On the day of the incident, Mr Darian had yelled, "You are completely bonkers, Clarke," as he whipped Joe's naked rump with a long brown cane in his locked office, an hour after Simpson and his bits of teeth had been collected from school by his parents.

Joe's parents didn't show. His father was detained in a Thai prison, and his mother's whereabouts were unknown that day. Her fortnightly social security payment had been due to arrive, and she liked a flutter on the horses. That was all Joe could tell Mr Darian.

Over the following months, the headmaster began keeping Joe in detention in his locked office. The detentions increased that winter when the curtain of night fell early. Joe was routinely placed inside a large seaman's chest that the headmaster used as a coffee table. Joe was only let out of the box when he agreed with the headmaster's demands for a type of silent obedience that Joe had observed in dogs that herded sheep on TV shows. Joe also learned in the headmaster's office that when things go undetected, they give the doer imagination. Joe couldn't believe what a grown man could do to him with a jar of petroleum jelly and the eels from the Grade 5 aquarium. And then Mr Darian would comb Joe's hair and send him home.

Lennie began waiting for Joe to leave Mr Darian's office. Lennie could do what he pleased after school because his widowed nanna, with whom he lived, could barely tell what day it was, let alone whether Lennie was home or not. He'd made a replica of himself using a party balloon and plastic bags stuffed with paper, which he dressed in his clothes and sat at the desk in his bedroom as if it was reading a book. His nanna would talk to it.

The flesh and bone Lennie started reading to Joe behind the scoreboard at the sports oval that spring when the days grew long again, and there was ample natural light to get through a chapter or two. Later, they used torches and candles in a shelter they rigged behind the scoreboard with a blanket and ropes. They first read a book titled *The Call of the Wild* by a bloke called Jack London. The boys wished they could have a dog like the book's hero, Buck, who was battered and abused by humans in the freezing North American Yukon during a gold rush. They would have shared with the dog the hot chips they bought from the local fish and chip shop with a few dollars given to Joe by the headmaster, who had the hairiest hands, most bulbous nose, and darkest whiskers that Joe and Lennie had ever seen. They vowed not to forget Mr Darian. Or his eels. Ever.

• • • •

IN THE KITCHEN, LENNIE opened a window to let in fresh air and clear his head of the fumes. As he turned, he saw the faded spine of George Orwell's *Animal Farm* on the bookshelf beside the fridge. While he'd not read the book for years, the story about how pigs enslave the other animals on the farm remained more vivid than the snakes that had just appeared on Joe's head. Now, thought Lennie, what was headmaster Darian's first name? All he could remember was that last year, during their last encounter with Mr Darian, they had cause to nickname him 'Squealer' after a pig in Orwell's book.

Lennie sat at the table and capped the travel bottle of bleach and alcohol. He opened his iPad and double-checked the time and the weather forecast. "Thirty minutes," he called to Joe.

Screeching erupted from a corner of the kitchen. Rawcus was awake. He strutted along the timber crossbar in his cage, which was hanging from a rope attached to a ceiling hook. The bird bobbed and weaved like a boxer dodging blows.

"Laast drinks!" Rawcus cried as loud and clear as a publican at closing time. "Laast drinks!"

Joe opened the fridge and extracted a can of beer. "Just a dash," he said to the bird, putting a splash of the amber fluid into the shallow tin on the floor of his cage. "You'll be in charge at home tonight, so you need to stay sharp."

Rawcus lifted his beak from the beer tin. "Sharp as a tack," he said. "I'm a model citizen, officer."

Joe drove the Firefly into the laneway behind their house and parked by the gate. He packed the van with the chloroform, the speargun, and the other items for the mission.

He dressed in a belted pair of shorts, his favourite T-shirt, a thick woolen sailing jumper, and rubber thongs for his feet.

Lennie had a hot shower and shaved and moisturised and perfumed his face and underarms. He dressed in his pinstripe suit trousers and white shirt, slinging his red silk tie around his neck.

"Very managerial," said Joe approvingly, watching Lennie knotting the tie in front of the wall mirror in the hallway.

Lennie's skin began to crawl as he buttoned the collar and tightened the knot. He slipped his jacket on and tucked his fat-rimmed reading glasses into an inside pocket.

"Joe, I've got a feeling something nasty and brown is about to hit our fan."

"When?" said Joe.

There was a knock at the front door.

It was a heavy knock that might hurt the knuckles of an ordinary person. It might not even be skin and bone striking the wooden door. It could be heavy metal.

The sun was down. Lennie flicked on the porch light and looked through the fish-eye security lens at three uninvited visitors.

5 – ROTTEN LUCK

TRIXIE Talaveda's round pink head – topped with spiked yellow hair – stared at Lennie through the lens. The parole officer was anchored between two hulking brown trunks of flesh upon which sat the Easter Island-statue-like heads of the Enoka brothers, Jona and Toku.

"Joe," whispered Lennie. "The parasites are here."

Joe retreated upstairs amid the second impatient wave of knocking. Lennie opened the door.

Trixie was almost as wide as she was tall, which is not very. A smoking cigarette dangled from the side of her mouth.

The Enokas grew up in the Solomon Islands in the South Pacific. They wobbled like overfed bulls as they shuffled behind her.

"Gidday," said Jona, the bigger of the brothers. "What are you all dressed up for, Lennie? Court appearance?"

"Job interview," said Lennie, bemused by the way Jona adjusted a waistline that resembled a kid's blow-up swimming ring filled with oil. When Jona lifted the fat in one spot, it just drooped in another. Lennie was grateful that Jona's gut was at least covered by a T-shirt.

"Aren't you going to invite us in, Lennie love?" Trixie rasped through her smoker's larynx. She exhaled the last of one into Lennie's face, then dropped the stub on the porch and ground it under her black ballet pump in an apparent display of good manners.

"No," said Lennie, admiring Trixie for her decision *not* to wear the red high heels from which she had toppled during her last visit, although she had been carrying a large open bottle of vodka at the time, which may have played a role in unbalancing her. "I'll be late for my appointment."

Joe appeared next to Lennie, carrying a backpack in his hand. It was loaded with a few kilograms of Mars Grass, the prime-grade resinous heads of their hydroponic crop, and some bundled, used banknotes.

"Have you boys been fishing recently?" said Trixie before coughing with a nasty bronchial rattle into a crumpled, once-white handkerchief.

Maybe it was the mention of fish, but Lennie noticed she had an unusually small mouth, thin-lipped and gap-toothed, like that of a blowfish. The porch light accentuated her wispy brown sideburns that were growing like weeds on the inflamed pink skin under her ears.

"Why do you ask?" said Lennie.

"Well," she croaked, wiping phlegm from her lips with her hanky before studying it briefly. "I read that a couple of fishermen had a very lucky break on a Balmain wharf a few days ago. You boys drop a line in the water over that way sometimes, don't you?'

"Yeah," said Lennie. "We read about that too, didn't we, Joe?"

"Mm," said Joe, thrusting the backpack into Jona's puffy paw.

Trixie said: "My law enforcement colleagues are looking for leads on that one. I'd put a little bit extra in the bag next month if I was you, Lennie. That's the sort of foresight that keeps you off the radar of the wrong sort of people."

Jona winked and slapped Lennie on the shoulder, closing off with a smile. Jona was missing a few teeth at the front grill of his mouth.

Toku looked Lennie up and down. "Job interview, my arse. You're a sad prick going on a Tinder date. Or Grindr. Yeah, probs both."

Toku tapped his pumpkin-shaped skull as if a light had turned on. "You're an electrician, aren't ya? Mr AC-DC. A switch hitter. Girl, boy, lady-boy. All the same to you, hey, Lennie."

The visitors cackled and walked into the street, climbing into the back of a shiny black four-wheel-drive. Two figures were waiting in the front seats, but the windows were tinted, blurring links in a chain of command that Lennie and Joe had given up trying to understand.

Joe closed the door. "Don't bite my head off, but you did add Trixie's and the Enoka boys' stuff to that phone from the wharf we sent to ASIO, yeah?"

"Does the Pope wear red slippers?"

Joe nodded. "We should shoot ASIO the rego of that chariot they just rode off in."

"Got it," said Lennie, who winked. "Let's pop it in the post, written on one of our special banknotes."

Trixie and her off-the-books bodyguards, the Enokas, had come for their monthly *tax*. The collectors didn't care if it was cash or kind. It just had to add up to five thousand dollars a month, based on a pre-agreed value for the Mars Grass that was adjusted quarterly for inflation, the calculation of the inflation being made by Trixie. If Lennie and Joe didn't pay? Or if they refused to grow the Mars Grass? Trixie and her colleagues would fit them up with crimes they didn't commit – and Lennie, with his history of offending the law, would be "re-caged" within hours, she regularly assured them.

Lennie checked the knot on his tie in the hall mirror, fingered his left ear where a chunk was missing from the outer rim, and recalled the title of a book he had found in the Silverwater Prison library.

Rotten Luck told about a man, who didn't believe in luck, who turned into a giant spider at night and ate strangers, who also didn't believe in luck, whom he encountered while they were camping in the bush.

Rotten luck is what, Lennie believed, led him to encounter the Enoka brothers and say goodbye to a piece of his left ear, which was bitten off by a pair of pliers wielded by Toku in the metalwork shop. That type of luck didn't end there: the Enokas and Lennie were released from Silverwater on the same day, into the care of Trixie Talaveda as a post-imprisonment gift from the State justice system.

Lennie brushed with his hands the lapels of his suit and buttoned up the jacket. He could lead a nation dressed like this. It was all in the look, leading with his right-side profile and his unbitten ear, of course. And with the reading glasses added – well, he as good as doubled his IQ in the eyes of the outside world.

Joe zipped closed two sports bags, one containing a change of clothes for Lennie: floral board shorts, a black T-shirt, and a black turtle neck jumper in case it got cold. They said goodnight quietly to Rawcus, who appeared to be dozing on the crossbar in his cage, his beer tin empty.

"Hang on," said Lennie. "Almost forgot my bloody hat." He bounded upstairs and collected a blond party wig from atop the head of a mannequin that stood beside his bedroom dressing table. The hair on the wig had been woven into a handful of rope-like braids.

They stepped into the street and climbed into the Firefly. Joe drove aimlessly for a few blocks, rolling his eyes until Lennie was convinced they were not being followed by Trixie and her gang, or anyone else. Then they headed for the Green Door Hotel.

Lennie opened his iPad as they motored, checking that the mobile connection to their home was working, and studied the screen.

"Oh, those new lenses work a treat," said Lennie, looking first through the camera mounted on an upper corner of their front porch, before checking on each of the rooms in their house. It had Lennie beat as to how Rawcus could snooze standing up on the swinging rod in his cage, especially after a few beers.

He replayed the recorded vision and soundtrack of Trixie and the Enokas making their collection.

"This is cinema quality, mate. Have a squiz." He held the screen up for Joe.

Joe prefered not crashing into other cars, so he kept his eyes on the road. "Just make sure you store that stuff in the heavens, or whatever you call it."

"I'm not a fan of the cloud," said Lennie. "You never know who's spying on your shit in there. But it's the best option we have, I guess."

Lennie touched the Jack in his pocket. The secure storage of this data was critical for their long-term health, including Rawcus's. If Trixie or her copper mates did decide to hit them with criminal charges – real or cooked up – then Lennie and Joe intended to take a crowd down with them.

First step: upload the recording of tonight's visit onto the Firefly Electrics Company's Facebook pages and its YouTube channel, along with other recordings Lennie has been collecting.

Plus throw some images on Instagram and TikTok. He thought "The Collectors" might make a good title for the show. Oh, and he'd flick a copy to that *City Daily* Crime Editor, Tom Steele, now that they'd become acquainted over the phone. The old-school newspaper scribbler might become useful.

As they crossed the Sydney Harbour Bridge heading towards the off-ramp to the Green Door Hotel, Lennie jiggled his tie and enjoyed the idea of Trixie and the Enokas explaining to anti-terrorism agencies how they were *not* linked to the $30 million of dirty money that was being shipped to Islamic State.

He hadn't been able to crack the PIN to open the apps on the phone that he'd found on the wharf. But he had looked up some Arabic symbols on the internet and scratched them, using a red felt-tipped pen, onto a few of the US dollar banknotes they'd gathered off the pier. He'd also written Trixie's and the Enoka's distinctive first names and phone numbers on the same notes, and wrapped them around the phone with an elastic band, before popping it in the envelope that they posted to ASIO. The Arabic symbols, when translated to English, said, *Allah is Great*. It mightn't be "go straight to jail stuff" for Trixi and Co, but they'd probably face a grilling under hot lights in a soulless room and have secret agents on their tails and bugs on their phones for months at least. Take that you pricks, thought Lennie.

"Here, OK?" said Joe, pulling into a loading zone downhill from the Green Door's main entrance.

Lennie put on his reading glasses and stepped out, crossing his fingers that the moustachioed turd was swilling copious amounts of stupifying chemicals in one of the bars.

• • • •

AS HE TOURED THE CORRIDORS of the Green Door, Lennie heard an ear-ripping rendition of the Queen song, *We Are The Champions,* reverberating from the rear lounge of the hotel. Lennie peeped into the room upon a rollicking crowd.

"Fuck me," he hissed, shaking his head at a mind-bending sight.

Michael O'Hay was standing on a karaoke stage, wearing a grey suit with his pink necktie loose, grasping a microphone on a long stand and pretending to be Freddie Mercury. The accountant thumped a fist on his chest and boomed "...no time for losers".

As far as Lennie could tell, the only likeness between Freddie and O'Hay was a caterpillar moustache – and even then, O'Hay's mo curled up at its ends instead of down.

The sweaty imitator ended his performance to the hoots and stomping feet of half a dozen business-suit-wearing men who were seated at a large table. O'Hay lifted a beer glass from the floor near his feet, took a bow, and strutted across the room to his red-nosed fans.

The accountant clinked drinks with each of the men who, Lennie calculated by the volume of their voices and the bobbling of their heads, must have been throwing amber suds down their throats and popping brain cells for hours. They'd probably attended a conference earlier in the day, and then back-slapped each other into a restaurant for an extravagant lunch paid for by someone's clients. This was Lennie's professional assessment based on his research in pub toilets.

O'Hay's mob was wearing matching baseball caps emblazoned with the logo of *YYY Investment Advisers.* Lennie circled near the table of the spittle-mouthed, wise men, pretending he was talking on his phone.

O'Hay's friends, arms over each other's shoulders, began chanting and stamping their feet like rowdy schoolboys.

Lennie jiggled an earlobe to be sure he was hearing the words right. Yep, there was no mistake: "If YOU don't eat...YOU don't shit! If YOU don't shit, YOU die! WE just eat 'n' shit...MO-NEY!"

Lennie sidled into a far corner of the bar, keeping an eye on O'Hay, and made a real phone call.

"Looks like he's been on the turps all day," he told Joe. "We're on."

"When?"

"He's walking out as we speak. Alone."

"If he's pissed, he might grab a taxi."

"Na. An arrogant prick like him will think he can drive and rat-run 'round the cops."

"He *is* a rodent," Joe agreed.

"Let's execute Plan A."

• • • •

ENTERING THE UNDERGROUND car park next to the Green Door, Joe shook his head at the eye-watering prices listed on the fee board. But this was an investment for the future.

He collected a ticket from a boom-gate dispenser and motored the Firefly below O'Hay's steel and glass office tower. Three levels down, he found the accountant's shiny red car parked in a private bay marked, *O'Hay Wealth Advisers*.

Joe scanned the walls and ceiling for CCTV – not a cracker. A man could get mugged down here and no-one would know, thought Joe. Given the fees the carpark owners gouged from the punters, this place was a bloody joke in terms of security. Fantastic!

He found an empty bay about half-a-stone-throw from O'Hay's Alfa Romeo and rolled the van in.

He grabbed his phone to call Lennie and give him the location, but because he was so far underground, there was no signal. My God, a man couldn't even make an emergency phone call down here. Fantastic! Joe checked the hunting knife in a sheath that was strapped to his belt and hidden under his sloppy black jumper. He locked the Firefly and headed for the lifts.

Standing in front of the elevator doors, he pressed Up. The doors opened. Lennie's face greeted him. There was a figure behind him. Lennie moved aside to let O'Hay stagger out.

"Gidday, mate," Joe said to O'Hay.

"Piss off," grunted the accountant, stuffing his hands in his trouser pockets, apparently searching for his car keys.

"Fair enough," said Joe, holding his hands up as if surrendering to a superior force.

Lennie followed O'Hay out. "Juice the rag," he whispered as he passed Joe. "I'll slow him down."

Squirts of adrenalin make Lennie bounce like a racehorse in a barrier waiting for the starter's bell. He touched the Jack in his trouser pocket.

O'Hay began circling, clutching his keys and pressing the buttons. His car tweeted and its parking lights flashed. O'Hay swayed in that direction. Lennie shadowed him. O'Hay dropped his keys. Lennie picked them up.

"I don't think you should drive, buddy," said Lennie, sliding the bridge of his reading glasses to the end of his nose and peering over the frames in a teacherly way.

"I'll be the judge," O'Hay grunted. "Give 'em..."

"You could kill someone."

"I'll kill you."

"Na," said Lennie. "Other way 'round."

"What?" O'Hay swayed. "I need a piss."

"What you need blockhead is a moral conscience."

"A fuckin' what?"

"Oh, look!" said Lennie. "Here it comes."

Joe, wearing a black beanie and wraparound sunglasses, strode at O'Hay from the side. O'Hay detected the lateral movement and turned towards Joe.

"Conscience?" muttered O'Hay, squinting at Joe as if he recognised him but couldn't quite place him.

Joe grabbed O'Hay's jacket collar with one hand and used his other to thrust a chemical-soaked cloth over his target's gristly nose and thin-lipped mouth. He had wanted to use petrol, but Lennie had insisted on his more sophisticated homebrew.

"Know where ya going?" Joe asked, smiling like he was watching a pre-recorded football game on TV where he knew what the fans and players didn't.

Joe wondered if O'Hay was seeing the same red, green, and yellow pigs he'd seen when he had tested Lennie's chloroform. The porkers had waltzed, faster and faster, spinning into a rainbow blur. O'Hay collapsed into Joe's arms.

They lay O'Hay on the floor in the back of the Firefly and put a charcoal-coloured pillowslip over his head before roping his hands and feet together so that the wealth adviser was in a foetal curl.

"What do you reckon?" said Lennie, slipping on a pair of latex gloves he had taken from his inside jacket pocket. "Do I look like an Alfa male, or what?"

"Don't speed," warned Joe, as Lennie marched towards O'Hay's car.

Joe drove the Firefly and followed Lennie. They dropped the Alfa in a street near to where the accountant moored his ocean-going yacht at the Birkenhead Point Marina in the city's inner harbour.

Together in the Firefly, they headed south along the coastal highway. If all went according to plan, they would reach their destination in about five hours.

Joe wound down his window to let fresh air buffet his face. "Been a strange few days," he said.

Lennie nodded. "Strange as a cat with two tails."

"I hope it doesn't grow a third tonight," said Joe.

• • • •

THE ROAD GREW EMPTY, straight, and dark, apart from the star belt of the Milky Way.

Lennie fingered his Jack and closed his eyes.

Thud! Joe felt the van lurch across the road into the oncoming lane; he wrestled the steering wheel back and rolled to a stop on his side of the tar.

Lennie opened his eyes and muttered, "The best-laid schemes of mice and fucking men, go oft awry..."

"What are you on about?" said Joe, opening his door.

"It just popped into my head," said Lennie, who decided now wasn't the time to explain the overlapping works of the American novelist John Steinbeck and the Scottish poet Robbie Burns, both of whom Aunty D had stuffed into his brain when he was younger. "What's up?"

"Busted tyre."

They moved with the synchronicity of a pit-stop crew to extract the spare tyre from the back of the van. Outside, Joe applied a cross-brace to loosen the wheel nuts on the busted one, while Lennie set to work lifting the van's undercarriage with a jack so they could remove it.

White lights winked at them, two sparkling dots in the distance, growing bigger.

"I reckon we've got about a minute," said Lennie.

"I'm fast," said Joe, "but not that fast."

Lennie figured that while the approaching car might stop, or it might not, a useful amount of risk mitigation could be achieved in less than sixty seconds. He padded as softly as a cat into the back of the van so as not to knock the Firefly off the jack, and pulled the pillowcase off O'Hay's head. He put an ear near to the accountant's frothy mouth. His breath stunk of bleach and vomit, but air flowed rhythmically in and out of his nose and mouth. Lennie threw a canvas drop-sheet over the numbers man, head and all. He extracted a knife in a sheath from a travel bag, stepped out onto the tar, and heaved the door shut.

"Here," he said, tossing the knife to Joe, who strapped it to the belt on his shorts.

Red and blue lights flashed atop the roof of the approaching vehicle. Its headlamps and a hand-guided spotlight illuminated Lennie and Joe like actors on a stage.

Lennie put a hand over his mouth and said to Joe, "This could be the cat with three tails. You set?"

Kneeling, Joe gripped the four-pronged wheel brace in one hand, and put his other hand behind his back to push the knife behind his bum and hide it under his jumper.

The police car stopped with its headlights so close to Joe and Lennie that they could feel the heat. A figure emerged from the passenger side door, the vehicle's beams creating a halo around the dark approacher.

"What's the problem, gentlemen," said a gravelly male voice.

"Flat tyre," said Lennie.

"That's terrible luck this time of night," said the man, keeping the headlights behind him so Lennie and Joe couldn't see his face. "Where are you boys going?"

"Milford," said Lennie, choosing the nearest town to the south. "Going spearfishing in the morning."

Lennie visualised Mr Lovecraft: the loaded, air-powered speargun was clipped to a rack on the inside wall of the van. Not a great option versus the copper's firearm, which he could see in the lawman's hip holster, but an option nonetheless. What a mess this would turn into if the night went truly pear-shaped. What would become of Rawcus, thought Lennie? There wouldn't be any winners from chaos here, except for O'Hay. He might escape justice yet.

Joe put the wheel brace at his feet and stood, slipping a hand behind his back and up his jumper to grip the handle of his knife.

"Got some ID, fellers?" said the officer.

Lennie took his driver's licence out of his wallet and nodded for Joe to follow suit. Joe let go of the knife and dug for the wallet in his shorts pocket with one hand, using the other to press a thumb tip into the fast-knotting scalp muscle in Mr Darian's favourite spot.

"A woman was assaulted near here last week when she was flagged down by a bloke with a broken car," the officer explained. "He was faking. And we haven't found him. So we're taking a special interest in this bit of track."

The officer took their licence cards and walked back to the patrol car.

Joe returned his hand behind his back. Lennie shook his head slowly at his friend, but he knew Joe's fuse was lit by the thought that O'Hay might win again with the assistance of the law of the land, the same law that had failed Aunty D, and countless thousands of others who'd been chewed up and shat out by the likes of O'Hay and his YYY's men pals. What had O'Hay called Aunty D in the emails they'd found? Yeah, "that dumbarse old hag?"

The police officer walked back and returned Joe's driver's licence. He turned to Lennie, "You got a special mention on our records, son. Are you being a good boy these days?"

"I like to think I'm a model citizen, officer."

"I'd like to think that too," the policeman said, handing Lennie his licence. "Have a good night."

O'Hay kicked the side of the van and groaned.

"You boys got other company?" snapped the officer, narrowing his eyes, apparently irritated at a perceived deception.

"He's sleeping," said Lennie.

It was silent on the highway, so the next wave of groans and convulsed gush of fluids inside the van was loud.

"Open the door," said the officer.

"You don't want us to do that," said Lennie, visualising Mr Lovecraft sitting in the rack on the Firefly's wall.

The officer was not for turning. He drew his pistol with both hands and aimed at Lennie's chest. "Open the fucking door!"

Joe grasped the handle of his knife. The other officer leaped from the patrol car and aimed his pistol at Joe.

"Grab some stars, you prick," the second lawman yelled. "On ya knees!"

Joe brought his hand back, empty, and lifted both arms casually beside his chest, yawning and stretching his back. He got on his knees, calculating the shifting odds of escaping. The coppers had guns, but his knife was handy. Drop and toss? It was dark outside the headlamp beams, and he and Lennie would have the element of surprise if they could dive into the black and fight from there. The spare wheel was beside him, not a bad shield, or missile. The four-pronged wheel brace could be a makeshift Ninja star. He saw that Lennie had the thumb of one of his hands stuffed inside his jeans pocket, his fingers hanging casually outside. Was touching a Jack his best idea?

Lennie took his thumb from his pocket and slung open the van door, holding his jacket sleeve over his nose and mouth to mask the stench he knew was coming. The first police officer held his pistol in one hand to cover Lennie, and plucked a flashlight from his waist belt with the other.

"Aww. Christ almighty," said the officer as he poked his head inside and trawled the van's innards with his flashlight. He reeled back, dry retching, waving his gun and light chaotically.

"Overdid it at the pub," said Lennie, who saw that O'Hay had managed to wiggle just his head out from under the canvas sheet. It was a stroke of luck not putting the pillowslip back on his head; maybe the Jack was working after all.

The accountant, eyes flickering, looked like he was tucked up in a sickbed. Yellow muck smeared his lips and moustache. O'Hay's hands were still roped to his ankles, so he couldn't lift them from under the canvas, which gave Lennie comfort.

The policeman's flashlight beam bounced about O'Hay's face, preventing the numbers-man from seeing that the carrier of the light was a could-be rescuer. Moreover, if there was any consciousness in O'Hay, fear had paralysed him into silence. And that was Lennie's gamble. O'Hay shut his eyes from the glare.

"Better you than me," the officer said, switching off his torch.

"We'll get him to our mate's place, clean him up, and we'll all have some kip," said Lennie, who slammed the sliding door shut.

The police made Joe breathe into an alcohol breath-tester. Zero.

As the officers drove away and Joe tightened the nuts on the fresh wheel, Lennie studied O'Hay's face under the Firefly's dim internal light. O'Hay opened an eye, and shut it.

"Sneaky weasel!" said Lennie. He grabbed a rag and gave O'Hay another sniff of bleach and alcohol.

"He might die before we get there," said Joe, starting the motor.

"That's up to the Gods," said Lennie. "Wind the windows down, will you?"

Joe lowered the windows and scratched his belly under his T-shirt. Gods, Joe thought, they were all bullshit artists, but some were more interesting bullshitters than others. On his T-shirt's ochre brown front was drawn Namarrgon, a grasshopper-like figure from the Aboriginal Dreamtime. Lightning Man, as some called him, wore stone axes on his head, and elbows and feet, which he used to split dark clouds and make lightning that he threw from the sky, sometimes at people when he got angry at what they had done. If Joe had to pick a god, he'd have this one.

• • • •

AT MILFORD, JOE STOPPED at a 24-hour garage where he bought a packet of cigarettes so they could stuff them into their nostrils to dull the nauseating stink in the van. Joe had seen this trick on TV, but he wasn't sure if you shoved the filter end in first, or the raw tobacco end. In the process of testing, Joe discovered that his nostrils were so big he could just bend the cigarettes in half and stuff both bits in each cavity.

"Want a light?" said Lennie, who flicked a cigarette lighter and waved the flame under Joe's beak.

Joe growled with a nasal twang, "With all the bloody fumes in here, you could blow us up."

In the back of the van, Lennie took his suit off and put on the board shorts, T-shirt, and turtle-neck jumper that Joe had packed for him. He tried the cigarette stink filter, but it burned, so he opted to roll the neck of his jumper up over his nose and mouth.

They speared into the night with O'Hay ranting something that sounded like the *Lord's Prayer* before he sang *Humpty Dumpty* badly.

• • • •

THE FIREFLY'S CLOCK showed 4.37 am when they parked near a deserted jetty under the stars. The boardwalk straddled the tideline of a sandy beach that curved along the still waters of mosquito-ridden and unpopular Halcion Bay.

On the horizon, darkness was battling the glow of the sun which was rising between rocky heads that lead to the open sea.

A wooden rowboat was tied to the jetty, bobbing under a cone of light cast from a sodium lamp on a pole. Barefoot, Joe carried O'Hay's canvas-wrapped body on his shoulder along the boardwalk and dropped the mumbling lump of meat and bone on the floor of the boat.

"Ow!" said Joe, as O'Hay's head clunked the inside wall of the dinghy.

O'Hay muttered through the cloth. "...had a big fall. All the king's horsies and all the king's men..."

Lennie climbed into the boat carrying his spear gun and the tightly packed sports bag. He sat at the back of the dinghy, O'Hay's head between his feet. Joe tossed him the mooring rope.

O'Hay snored.

Joe sat in the middle seat and rowed into the bay to where two yachts were floating side-by-side, bound by ropes and separated by car tyres. They were anchored by chains to a concrete block that Lennie and Joe had dropped on the seabed a few years ago.

The smallest yacht had brass letters screwed into its white-painted mahogany prow – letters that Lennie had assured Joe spelled *Flamingo Sky*. The other yacht, about twice as big as theirs, had *Make Hay* painted on its sleek, fibreglass hull.

At the close-up sight of *Make Hay*, Lennie growled, "It was like sailing a bloody plastic bucket with an umbrella for a spinnaker."

He'd navigated *Make Hay* solo down the coast on a nasty ocean two nights ago, after he and Joe had double-kayaked to a jetty of the high-security Birkenhead Point Marina in Sydney Harbour after midnight. They'd freed *Make Hay* from its chains using a diamond-bladed hacksaw that emitted little noise.

While Lennie was at sea, Joe had motored the Firefly down to Halcion Bay, carrying the flat-pack of steel mesh in the back which he loaded onto the *Flamingo* and roped to its foredeck. By the time Lennie arrived, chilled to the bone, Joe was waiting with a mug of hot coffee and toasted crumpets spread with butter and Vegemite.

This morning, as the eye of an orange sun peeped over the horizon, the *Flamingo* put-putted through the heads with Lennie at the helm and Joe unfurling a spinnaker to make use of a slight wind so they could cut the motor in the open sea. They tugged O'Hay's boat on a rope.

"Do you think anyone saw us?" said Lennie.

"Didn't see a soul. What's on your mind?"

"The bicycle that was leaning on the toilet block wall."

"Gotcha," said Joe. "We shoulda looked inside."

6 – MONEY TREES

WITH THE WIND at their backs, the sailors were soon alone and slicing through green water under blue sky.

Joe looked skyward. The vapour trails of two jetliners crisscrossed like chalk lines drawn by a giant hand. They reminded him of school. And his old headmaster. Joe batted away the nausea that arrived along with an image of Mr Darian's hairy nostrils as if seen under a magnifying glass. Joe turned his gaze to O'Hay who was unfurled from his canvas and curled on the rear deck near the *Flamingo's* wheel. He was gape-mouthed and snoring, flapping his lips now and then.

The accountant's wrists remained bound with rope and connected to his ankles. O'Hay was still wearing, after a fashion, his grey business suit, white shirt, and pink tie. His cream-coloured socks had almost slipped off his shoeless feet.

"What do you reckon he had for dinner last night?" said Joe, looking at the orange stains on the front of O'Hay's jacket. "Chicken Tikka?"

"Whatever it was, it doesn't look like he chews properly," said Lennie. "What a waste of those expensive teeth."

So, Lennie thought, this is the cock-in-a-suit who helped Aunty D sell her corner shop, and then helped himself and his mates to cash in on the apartment development on the site. And then he took her remaining savings. Oh, yeah. That final act was an inspired sleight of hand.

Lennie nodded to no-one in particular. He had to admire O'Hay's appetite for hard work and his ingenuity. Oh, and his sense of timing...

• • • •

DURING THE ALMOST SIX months it took Aunty D to sell her shop, and for O'Hay to sprinkle fairy dust in her eyes about what to do with the proceeds, Lennie and Joe had been island-hopping around Western Indonesia and the South Pacific, following Lennie's release from parole. Aboard *Flamingo Sky*, they had navigated calm seas and stormy, lived off fish caught on their bamboo rods, and feasted on tropical fruit and duty-free booze.

On their return home, making their first visit to Aunty D's new retirement village flat, Lennie and Joe had sensed a kink or three in her mind. Though she insisted, as always, that she was "good as gold, my beautiful boys".

On their next visit, some of her new neighbours said they were worried that she slept most of the day and walked the village streets at night.

"Why walk at night?" Lennie had asked her.

"It's safer," she replied.

Lennie had scratched his shaved head. In some ways Aunty D was right. A lot of weirdos don't like the dark. Lennie gave her a wristwatch with a GPS tracker inside it, just in case she strayed.

"She's depressed," ventured some old friends, although no-one could provide a convincing explanation about the downward spiral of her usually sunny disposition, apart from parroting on about the naturally occurring ravages of age on peoples' minds and bodies.

Lennie next observed that she had given up reading books and newspapers, as well as betting on the horses. She watched more TV, and listened to talk-back radio which she had always loathed. He secretly listened to her one morning through the flywire-screen back door when he came to visit.

He recognised the voice of a male know-it-all who was blabbering in the kitchen. Aunty D was trying unsuccessfully to get a word in edgeways with another man who was also in the room.

When Lennie looked through the screen, he saw that Aunty D was physically alone. But the radio was raging. She was talking to the strangers' voices about the high price of milk and lamb chops, while the strangers talked to each other about what a twit the Prime Minister was. Then she stepped closer to the radio and asked the talk-back jock if he wanted sugar and milk in his tea.

Around that time, she had started guzzling casks of white wine from midday, and washing down a dizzying array of medicines. Lennie had researched on the internet the stuff he found in her bathroom cabinet. There was Alprazolam for relief from the terrors of the day, and Triazolam to sleep at night. Her General Practitioner, Dr Finlay, told Lennie to bugger off when he asked the doc for his thoughts on Aunty D's state of mind and questioned his treatment methods. The medicine man spouted something to him about "doctor-patient confidentiality".

One evening, for her birthday, Lennie took her a tub of her favourite Taggiasca olives from Liguria in Italy. Small brown ones with a nutty tang.

"They are very expensive," Aunty D said.

Lennie was embarrassed. He'd purchased them on special. "Don't worry about it."

"Mangos too."

"Mangos?"

"Have you not heard of money trees, love?"

"Happy birthday," said Lennie, topping up his aunt's flute with the alcohol-free, sparkling pink wine. He was now in no doubt she had flipped her lid.

"You don't know what I mean," she said. And she told Lennie about her recent dealings with O'Hay, whom she had entrusted with her finances as her accountant and investment adviser for more than ten years.

"He was like Dr Finlay, Lennie. I told him everything. I made a mistake, love. I've been too embarrassed to say."

Three weeks after her revelations during that fleeting moment of clarity, Aunty Doreen was dead from what Dr Finlay called "a cerebrovascular accident" on a crosswalk near the local shops.

At first, Joe thought "Sir Rebro Vascular" was some lunatic English toff who drove his car into Aunty D.

It boiled down to a thing the doc called "a stroke" from a burst blood vessel in the brain.

They got a pet the day she died. Aunty D had called it Laurie.

"Giss a kiss, love. Giss a kiss, love," the bird had cried as Lennie carried his aunt's cockatoo in its cage into the Firefly. The animal, whom Lennie and Joe had known since it was a baby that was found lost with its wings clipped in the beer garden of the pub, didn't shut up.

By the time they got home, it had a new name. Rawcus was born.

A few days later, they had collected Aunty D's belongings from the flat that O'Hay had helped her buy. Lennie had stuffed paperwork – legal contracts and the like, including some thoughtful letters from O'Hay to the old lady – into a shopping bag.

"Homework," he said to Joe about the contents of the bag as they drove away. It contained information about Aunty D's so-called *money trees*.

• • • •

STANDING ON THE DECK of *Flamingo Sky*, Joe threw a red plastic bucket with a rope tied to its handle over the side and dragged it full of water. He hauled it in.

He and Lennie shuffled around to make sure the sun was precisely behind them as they stared down at O'Hay. They intended to give him nothing more of them to see than their halos, at least for the time being. The breeze was dropping, the water's surface turning glassy and humping with the swell.

Joe hurled the contents of the bucket over O'Hay, whose body writhed and whose eyes popped open.

"Look at you," said Lennie, shaking his head at the spluttering man. "You've got no fucking idea who we are, have you?"

O'Hay struggled and sat up, bum on the deck with his lower back against a stainless steel post of the wire safety rail. He shook his head in agreement.

"Doreen Dixon," said Lennie. "The name ring a bell?"

O'Hay appeared to pass out from the shock, falling to one side, although he landed in slow-motion on the deck shoulder-first, absorbing the impact on his muscles, before bringing his head more gently to rest, eyes closed.

Lennie and Joe rolled their eyes.

"Why don't we let sleeping weasels lie," said Lennie, "while we find the right venue."

They cruised beyond sight of land.

Lennie turned into the soft breeze until the sails were empty of air. Joe tossed the parachute of the sea anchor overboard. When the *Flamingo* was still and her sails furled and tied off, Joe stepped to the stern and pulled the rope that connected to O'Hay's boat.

The gunwales of *Make Hay* and *Flamingo* kissed.

7 – MR LOVECRAFT GETS RESTLESS

JOE JUMPED onto the deck of *Make Hay* and descended into the cabin for the fifth time in the last twenty-three minutes, according to a wall-mounted clock.

The frequent sight and sound of the clock's second-hand clicking around its face reminded Joe of a book Lennie tried to read to him last week called *A Brief History of Time,* which was written by a strange-looking Pommy bloke in a wheelchair who was an expert on the birth of the planets and stars. And like some stars, the bloke was now dead. But his light shone on in his book, according to Lennie.

The *History of Time* story didn't seem brief at all to Joe and it made less sense to him the longer it went on. So they didn't get past page five. Lennie kept going at the book on his own at the kitchen table while sampling his homemade chloroform for quality and effect, and subsequent dosage calculations for O'Hay.

Joe had turned on the telly, watched football, and drank beer with Rawcus, but the damn time yarn had dug its claws into Joe's brain and kept making him think about where time goes, and about getting old, and what happens when you die. All the stuff he was usually pretty good at ignoring.

Aboard *Make Hay,* the time-tracker clicked annoyingly in Joe's ear as he worked on a job that involved wires and batteries and ammonium-nitrate. He hoped it wouldn't be the last thing he did on earth and tried to concentrate on the probable and not the possible.

On the deck of *Flamingo*, O'Hay, with stringy snot clinging to his handlebar moustache, opened his eyes slightly, and quickly squeezed them shut.

"Having a nice day?" said Lennie, who was pissing into the sea, unsure why he changed his mind about watering the accountant instead, wondering if he was getting soft. If this was a newly emerging propensity for mercy, he wasn't sure he liked it.

Joe emerged from the cabin of *Make Hay*. "All set, mate," he called to Lennie.

He jumped across to *Flamingo's* deck, firing a leer at O'Hay that made the accountant flinch.

Lennie studied O'Hay and did a pretend moustache curl. "You really are Mr Style, Micky. I mean, what possessed you to grow that at your age?"

O'Hay's face crinkled as if puzzled by the question.

"You do realise, don't you," said Lennie, "that you look like a cardboard-cut-out villain. Or do you think it gives the little girls you're so fond of a tickle?

O'Hay farted and burped. The stench of vomit and bleach floated in the still air.

Joe pinched his nose with the pads of his thumb and index finger. "With a mo like that, I reckon Mr O'Hay might be in one of those barbershop singing mobs."

"Of course," said Lennie, boarding Joe's train of thought. "Micky, what was that witty ditty you and your wise mates belted out at the Green Door last night?"

O'Hay tried to shake the snot from his nostrils, but it wouldn't let go.

Lennie faked grabbing a karaoke microphone. "*We are the champions, we are the champions*...hang on, wrong song."

Lennie scratched his forehead. "Ah, it was an original, wasn't it, Micky? Remember?"

O'Hay groaned.

Lennie stomped a foot and let rip. "*If YOU don't eat...YOU don't shit. If YOU don't shit, YOU die. Wee, just eat 'n' shit...Mo-ney!*"

O'Hay grizzled. "We were just having fun."

"Well," said Lennie, "Fun's over. You're about to spend the day in court."

O'Hay appeared puzzled. "Court?"

"Here's a clue," said Lennie. "It's not tennis."

Joe descended into the *Flamingo's* cabin and returned with a large drink cooler that he sat on the deck. He pulled out two cans of beer and tossed one to Lennie. Joe snapped his ring-pull, had a few gulps, and wiped his brow with the back of a hand.

"Stinks down there," he said, pointing at O'Hay's yacht. "Like a sewer."

"Let's give it a flush, hey," said Lennie, who reached into his board shorts pocket and extracted a phone. "I love Bluetooth." He pressed a button.

There was a dull thud like a faraway firework. The sea around *Make Hay* rippled. The boat lurched slowly to starboard. The mining explosive and its detonator appeared to have done their job and blown a hole through its hull.

O'Hay spluttered, wrenching against his ropes, "You fucking morons have just sunk a f..."

"What's that?" said Lennie.

O'Hay swooned. The sun was hot.

Lennie and Joe removed their jumpers and shirts to absorb some rays. Lennie scratched a black tattoo of a hypnotic wheel that was stained into the skin over his left breast.

The trio watched in silence, Lennie and Joe sipping beer, until *Make Hay* went tail up and sunk below the surface with a frothy burp.

"Jesus, Micky," Lennie said, turning to O'Hay. "Lucky you weren't on board, hey?"

O'Hay looked at Lennie, puzzlement giving way to a weak smile, as if it was dawning on him that if his captors wanted to kill him, they could have sunk him on the boat just now.

"Is that a look of hope I can see on your face, Micky?" said Lennie. "It's fundamental to existence, hope. I'm sure you know that. Take it away and a lot of people lose the will to live."

O'Hay squinted. "What do you want?"

"Your full attention for a start."

The surface humped; swell lines rocked the boat. On the horizon, streaks of pink and grey were emerging on the dark blue canvas of the sky.

Lennie said to Joe, "Let's have a smoko before we start the trial."

O'Hay blurted, "Trial?"

Lennie smiled at their snotty-faced passenger and pulled sinus-cleansing sea air through his nostrils and deep into his lungs. He admired the dawn sky which now had a purplish tinge amid the pink and grey. He chuckled; Delling appeared to be using a spray can this morning.

Joe stepped into the cabin and sat on a bench seat beside a narrow table. He started rolling a Mars Grass reefer. As he licked the gum on the cigarette paper and sealed his trumpet, a newspaper on the seat attracted his eye.

"Hey," Joe yelled. "Check this out!"

"What?" Lennie called.

Joe immediately regretted his attention-seeking shout. He didn't reply.

Lennie swung down into the cabin, wondering if Joe had discovered a leak that could sink their plans.

This was a tricky moment for Joe. He kept his mouth shut. Luckily the newspaper article that had triggered his spontaneous outburst included something that any idiot could understand: a photograph. The written word was another matter, and the truth was that Joe had been attending adult literacy classes at night school – while telling Lennie he was weightlifting at a gym.

Now that Joe was mastering the rudiments of reading, he had become afraid that Lennie would find out and that his feelings would be hurt. Worse still, such a discovery by Lennie might do terrible damage to their "dysfunctional co-dependency" as Trixie Talaveda called it. Joe had originally gone to literacy classes intending, one day, to relieve his friend of a burden. But now Joe found himself snared in a limbo of guilt and confusion. *To read, or not to read.* Joe handed the newspaper to Lennie, just as he had done for years.

Joe lit his smoke, and Lennie read aloud:

The sailor savaged by a shark in Sydney Harbour has been named as Able Seaman Clearance Diver David Palmer.

The 29-year-old lost one leg and part of a hand in the incident shortly before 7am at the navy base near the iconic Harry's Cafe de Wheels at Woolloomooloo.

Seaman Palmer, of the Royal Australian Navy's Clearance Diving Team, was carrying out an anti-terrorism exercise...

"Poor bastard," said Joe, blowing smoke, watching it travel up the steps towards the outside. He noticed that O'Hay had wiggled across the deck to the hatch hole and was staring down at him with a pleading smile.

"I don't mean you, bozo," said Joe, standing.

Lennie grabbed the sports bag off the table and his speargun. Joe led him up to the deck. Lennie sat atop a flat timber strut fixed between two safety rail posts and looked down at O'Hay who had wiggled back against another post. "What good have *you* ever done for other people, Micky?"

O'Hay said nothing.

"Yeah," said Lennie, taking the joint offered by Joe. "I thought that would be the case."

O'Hay groaned. "What...what do you guys want from me?"

"We're getting to that," said Lennie.

"Whacko!" yelled Joe. "Look!"

A humpback whale was breaching the sea's surface a stone's throw away. It puffed a misty cloud through its breathing hole and flashed its broad, black back. Plunging into the briny, it signed off with a thunderous wallop of its glistening tail that wet the mariners.

"Magic," said Joe, wiping seawater from his eyes and sniffing the creamy salt of whale oil in the spray, fighting the urge to dive in.

"Smoko's over," said Lennie, flicking his water-spattered reefer overboard.

"You blokes want money, is that what this is about?" croaked O'Hay.

"Ever explored the occult?" asked Lennie, who noticed the accountant was staring at the hypnotic wheel tattoo on his breast.

He pulsed his pectoral muscles. O'Hay's head circled, his eyes appearing transfixed by the spinning wheel.

"I'm a devout Christian. Honest to God," O'Hay insisted.

"Wrong answer," said Lennie, fondling his spear gun. "We had another community leader out here. A religious man too, so he said. A priest. Spanish name. Taught me Sunday school. Anyway, we let him loose to give him choices, and he jumped over the side and tried to swim for it. It wasn't an option we offered.

"So I had to fire Mr Lovecraft here into him – and haul him back on the rope. I felt like I was that Queequeg feller from Moby Dick. You know the harpoon guy, all covered in mysterious tatts? Except I don't shoot whales."

O'Hay's eyebrows arched and his jaw dropped, his face freezing as if locked upon a horrifying vision.

"Maybe I'm joking," said Lennie.

O'Hay relaxed.

"Or maybe I'm not."

A dark patch appeared in the groin of O'Hay's grey designer suit.

Lennie laid Mr Lovecraft at his feet and unzipped the sports bag. He removed a stainless-steel-headed axe as if he was extracting nothing more unusual than a beach towel.

"Bought this just for you, Micky. Brand spanking new. It's a present from good old dead Aunty Doreen and some friends of hers who've chipped in from the grave too. Now, what happens next is up to you, in part."

Joe sat on a timber strut between the safety rail posts, opened a fresh beer, and yawned.

Lennie gripped the flat back of the axehead and loomed over O'Hay. "Move at your peril."

He kneeled and used the razor-sharp blade to slice the ropes that bound the trembling accountant.

"Get the Armani off," Lennie said to O'Hay.

"Why?"

"Chop, chop."

O'Hay stripped to his shirt and underpants, folding his suit neatly and stacking it on the deck.

"I've got to give it to you, Mr O'Hay," said Joe, wiping beer foam from his mouth and shaking his head. "You really think you're going to wear that again, don't you?"

"Birthday suit, please, Micky," said Lennie, who sat on the strut opposite Joe, grasping the top of the axe handle with both fists, impatiently tapping the tool's glistening head on the wooden deck. He wondered how much Viking blood was actually coursing through his veins. He certainly felt like a Viking right now. He should have one of those ancestry DNA tests. But what if it's zero? Na, not worth the risk. What if his Norwegian nanna wasn't really his nanna? Na, he'd opt for blissful ignorance. His Sunday school teacher, Father Francesco, had called him a mongrel bastard during their final encounter. Francesco probably had inside knowledge, him being a Catholic big-hitter who gathered gossip in the confessional and spread it when it suited him.

O'Hay removed his shirt and pushed down his underpants, hiding his gristly manhood with his bony hands.

"And the watch," said Lennie, who held out an open palm into which O'Hay placed it.

Lennie resumed, "You know what they do to thieves in Saudi Arabia, Micky? That's right; they cut off their hands. But given we are in a different jurisdiction, maybe we ought to knock off the little thing between your legs that was so fired up in your car under that camphor laurel with the girl the other night. Though it's in hiding now. Look, Joe! Talk about beating a hasty retreat..."

Joe retied the accountant's ankles with plastic zip-locks. He did O'Hay the favour of tying his wrists in front of him, enabling the nude man to sit on his bum with his back against a rail post in sunlight.

Joe studied goosebump-skinned O'Hay and spoke to Lennie. "He looks like a plucked chook, don't you think, now he's got no feathers on?"

Lennie swung the handle of the axe onto one of his shoulders. O'Hay's eyeballs threatened to pop from their sockets.

"Ah, don't you worry, Micky. You're not worth eating. Not by us, anyway. But you can do some good for once in your life. We're gonna post the cash from your wallet to the Red Cross. You've ruined your clothes, though, you grub."

Joe stuffed O'Hay's clothes into a black garbage bag.

"And what are we going to do with this fancy watch of yours?" said Lennie, who read from its back: *To Michael. Love Always, Possum.*

"Who's *Possum*?" said Lennie.

"My wife."

"So romantic," said Lennie, "marrying a marsupial."

"You pervert," squeaked O'Hay. "It's her nickname."

"Pull the other leg."

"OK. I gave it to myself."

"That makes sense," said Lennie, who threw the watch to Joe, who tucked it in a pocket of his shorts.

"Where is our fashionista's other shoe?" said Lennie, tossing Joe a camel-coloured slip-on with leather tassels.

"Uh, oh," said Joe. He scanned the deck for a few seconds, looking over the sides into the water, then climbed into the cabin. He returned moments later and turned his empty palms up.

Lennie touched the Jack in his pocket. "Never mind. It'll turn up. Or it's sunk."

Above them, a patch of cloud moving on a high wind blocked the sun. O'Hay shivered.

"Weather's on the turn," observed Joe, who put on the T-shirt that he had kept tucked in a back pocket of his shorts.

"OK. Showtime," said Lennie, who unbuttoned his board shorts. He turned to O'Hay.

"I think it's only fair that we face each other man-to-man," said Lennie. "No secrets. We're gonna get to the naked truth."

"This is nuts," said O'Hay.

"Ha," said Lennie, pulling off his shorts.

"Jesus Christ, you're not going to rape me, are you?" O'Hay squirmed.

"Do I look like the son of God to you?" said Lennie, who stroked his chest and arms. His lithe body had not a hair in sight. He had shaved it last night before he donned his business suit. It made his skin easy to clean, and things could soon become very messy.

Lennie tapped his forehead. "Ah, almost forgot. There's something I do need to pop on first, merely to establish jurisdiction in these proceedings."

Joe smiled at the accountant. "How's your imagination going, Mr O'Hay?"

Lennie stepped down into the cabin. Through a porthole, he watched lightning strobe inside fluffy grey balls floating above the seaside horizon. Upon the table sat his blond wig with its hair woven into braids. He put it on his head and looked in a mirror. "Good morning, your Honour."

Back on deck, Lennie sat on the drink cooler and placed the head of the axe between his spread feet, grasping the end of the handle with both hands. He faced O'Hay.

The accountant appeared close to tears. "What the hell is going on?"

"I know it might be a little confusing for you, being off your patch, out of your power zone. Whatever you want to call it. Think of me as the prosecutor in your case. You are mounting your own defence. My companion here is an officer of the court."

"Who's the judge then?" said O'Hay.

"The judge is out there," said Lennie, pointing to the sky and then to the sea. "Oh, and the judge is in here too." Lennie clutched the axe handle between his kneecaps and pointed his index fingers simultaneously at his head and Joe's head.

"What's the charge?" said O'Hay, his eyes narrowing as if he was grasping the game.

"Let's start with thievery, Micky. Industrial-scale thievery. Then there are multiple charges of destruction of people's lives for the purpose of you being able to drive a nicer car, boat, etcetera. You get the drift, I trust. Oh, and you've mentally tortured your wife and physically molested your daughters. And you've done the same to young women in your employ, minus the physical bruising. Quite a track coverer, aren't you?"

"You can't prove any of that."

"Mm. How do you plead to unscrupulous cleverness then? Guilty, or not guilty?"

"You really are fucked in the head."

"That's better, Micky. Show us some of that trademark spunk of yours. The figurative stuff only, if you don't mind."

O'Hay spat the saliva string from his lips.

"Officer," said Lennie. "Please pass me the evidence bag."

Joe stepped into the cabin, and returned with a briefcase that he handed to Lennie.

Lennie said, "Is it true that you told Doreen Dixon that money grew on trees?"

"Of course not."

Lennie opened the briefcase.

"*Golden Garden*," said Lennie, plucking out a glossy brochure. "What a cracking name. I'll paraphrase what's inside it – for the economy of the court's time. This document is chock-a-block with dazzling graphs and numbers, promising investors a sure-fire path to wealth and security. Other brilliant minds were involved in its preparation, not just yours, Micky. I acknowledge that. Some of the nation's finest financial brains, as a matter of fact, global brains even."

O'Hay burped.

"Now," said Lennie. "I want to read to the court from this item. It is a note I recorded during an interview with Doreen Dixon. So she is speaking from the grave, if you like, as a few of today's witnesses will be, in fact.

"She said that you, Micky, licked jam off your thumb at her kitchen table, drew a pretty diagram on a piece of paper, and said: *Look, Doreen. You just put your money in here. Then we grow the trees for you – olives, mangos, and whatnot – and when the product is sold, the money pours back into your bank account. Hey, presto! You are set for life. There really are money trees.*

"That's a lie," O'Hay spluttered.

"Oh, I know it's a lie, Micky," said Lennie. "I just want to know if you said it."

Lightning fizzed through the blackening plumes on the horizon and thunder grumbled.

Lennie looked at the sky and mused, "Funny, isn't it, Micky. Life can be just like the weather. Perfect one moment, terrifying the next."

Thunder cracked. O'Hay's flesh wobbled like grey jelly. "What are you going to do to me?"

"The court's still in session, Micky. You're jumping the gun."

"Gun?" said O'Hay.

Joe, employing a flattened hand upon his brow as a sun visor, kept an eye looking out to sea for the return of his whale, but he kept his other eye and his ears focussed on the court, not wanting to neglect his official duties and make the prosecutor cranky. He also scanned the sea for troublemakers, such as other sailors. He loved being a scout, though he was always grateful that as kids, he and Lennie never had enough money to become the official types who wore khaki uniforms and red scarves with wooden toggles. They weren't inclined to add scoutmasters to the male role models they already had wanting to hold their hands.

Lennie adjusted his slipping wig. "So what happened to the money trees?"

O'Hay shook his head. "It's not my fault they failed to make a profit. Life is full of risk. Your aunty knew that."

"The truth is, Micky, when some bright sparks woke up to your money tree bullshit, and Mr and Mrs New Customer stopped putting cash into the projects, the beast stopped eating and shitting money, as you wise guys sing it. The monster died. And amid the festering stink, when you raced away from the carcass in your red

Alfa with a little hard-on in your pants, banks called in their loans and took away peoples' homes. Old folks lost their retirement savings. Small businesses and marriages were shattered. But nothing bad happened to you – you took all your commissions upfront. And banked them. Clever, Micky. Impressive."

O'Hay sniffled. "It's no crime being smart."

"Nor is it a crime being a businessman, Micky. I mean, Joe and I have nothing against the economics of supply and demand. We're capitalists ourselves. We have an electrician's business, and we do some professional gardening."

"OK," said O'Hay. "We are on the same page then. We are all entrepreneurs."

"We are all sailors too, Micky. But there was something we couldn't find on your boat."

"What's that?"

"A compass."

"I had a compass."

"I mean a moral compass."

"Get fucked," foamed O'Hay.

"Ha. That's the boy," said Lennie. "Remember, Don Gerrity?"

"No." O'Hay dropped his head, apparently woozy.

"He was your client, Micky. Aunty D's lawn bowls partner. Surely you remember jolly Don. He was a barber. Indigenous feller, one of the Stolen Generations. He gassed himself in his car. You don't recall?"

"Excuse me, officer," Lennie said to Joe. "I think the accused is nodding off."

Joe threw the red bucket on a rope into the sea, and hurled the contents over O'Hay, whose body bucked.

"Now, where was I," said Lennie. "Yes. Mr Donald Gerrity. He thought the life insurance company would pay his death benefit to his disabled daughter, Pauline. We went to school with Pauls, didn't we, Joe? Good old, Don. He taught us to sail as kids, on a little Laser he could put on his roof rack..."

Joe bongo drummed on the bottom of the upturned bucket to get the prosecutor back on track.

"I digress into sentimentality. Apologies to the court," said Lennie. "Mr Gerrity had done his homework. If he killed himself less than thirteen months after taking out the life insurance policy, the insurance company had no obligation to pay.

"But he had been paying the premiums on the policy for nearly two decades, so his daughter was in for the money. You, Micky boy, were in the super-know because you had set up the policy for him, and you took a regular trailing commission from the insurer out of Mr Gerrity's payments. It probably paid for those fancy teeth of yours.

"What Mr Gerrity failed to appreciate was that if the policyholder had any undeclared history of mental illness, the insurance company could deny payment. Of course, he had confided his anxiety and panic attacks to you, Micky, because they were caused by your dodgy money trees. And what did you do with this information?"

O'Hay looked out to sea.

"It was brilliant," said Lennie. "After his death, you dobbed him to the insurance company, and took a spotter's fee for saving the insurer a couple of hundred thousand bucks."

O'Hay arced up. "If I've broken the law, put me in front of a proper court. You're going to jail for the rest of your stinking lives for this charade. Kidnapping and torture are serious offences."

"Oh, is that all you think we are going to do to you?" said Lennie.

O'Hay swooned. "I think I'm having a heart attack!"

Joe took his beer can from his lips and said reassuringly, "No worries, Mr O'Hay. We've got some jumper leads and a truck battery. If you keel over, I'll give you a heart starter."

Lennie continued, "Did you know that when the media said the money tree projects were *Ponzi's*, Aunty D thought it was a new type of pizza chain?"

O'Hay panted. "The lawmakers, the regulators," he gasped. "They disagreed they were Ponzi Schemes."

"Oh, the good old law," said Lennie. "It's a terrific little pal of yours, and your mates, Micky. Now, where was I? Oh, yes...what did you tell Doreen when she asked you for help to save her retirement flat, which was the last thing she owned, or part-owned to be accurate?"

"I did all I could," said O'Hay, who cocked an ear as if he might be hearing something in the distance. His eyes darted, suggesting accelerating electrical activity in his cranium.

Lennie took another sheet of paper from his briefcase and peered down at O'Hay. He felt for a moment like the bespectacled beak who, wearing a blond wig and black robe, sent him to Silverwater Prison for tossing a condom full of red house paint that burst upon the Archbishop of Sydney. *You cannot fight perceived injustice with a crime of your own,* the judge had lectured Lennie, whose prior conviction for vandalising a church didn't help in his sentencing.

Lennie said to O'Hay, "You must have had a nice boozy lunch before you tapped out this email to your lawyer."

O'Hay groaned. Lennie read from the sheet of paper.

To Ian Hedland & Partners – Solicitors.

Hi Ian – the old hag is still on my case. I want you to fire off a letter on your fanciest law firm letterhead and terrorise the crap out of her. Tell her I've found an old bill she hasn't paid. Make it $4,920.95. So it looks like I didn't cook it up. And for the record, I didn't. She owes me for the stress.

Yours, Michael.

PS: That new girl you have on your front desk. You should bring her to drinks next Friday night.

Joe turned to Lennie and pointed at grumbling black plumes being lashed by white flashes on the horizon. "Someone is giving us a hint to wrap this up. I reckon we have about thirty minutes."

Lennie turned to O'Hay and saw a man who told the truth in the same way as the hard-fingered priest, Father Francesco, who swore on the Bible in front of the Bishop that he'd only given six-year-old Leonard Larson a lift home from Sunday school in his car to save him walking in the blistering summer heat. He "most certainly did not" park under a tree and "touch" Leonard, as the psychologically unstable child had claimed. The Bishop agreed that Lennie had an "evil streak". In the wash-up, Lennie was taken "to be cleansed" on a Sunday school camping trip by Father Francesco and his friends. In the tent at night, Lennie convinced himself it was just a dream, a psychological perspective that the faceless men helpfully suggested he adopt, while they poured a fluid into his mouth that burned his throat and made him dizzy. Then they tag-teamed each other to express their "love" for him. Lennie shut up about it. No-one was interested in the weird dreams of a deranged child. For several years afterward, Lennie was taken on regular camping trips by Father Francesco where he had similar dreams.

••••

O'HAY LOOKED SKYWARD, studying the lengthening vapour trail of a passenger jet.

"Oh, Micky, Micky, Micky," said Lennie. "The more we've come to know you over the past few months, the more transparent you have become. Sort of like a jellyfish. You'd love to be on that jet, wouldn't you? And you almost made it, hey! We arrived in the nick of time. Joe, can you show the court Exhibit G, please?"

Joe stepped into the cabin, and emerged waving a shiny gold brick about the size of a phone.

"You fuckers!" O'Hay spluttered, arching his back and furiously fighting his shackles.

Lennie said, "Your acting skills are A-class, Micky. You barely blinked when you saw *Make Hay* sinking into Davy Jones Locker. Although you did almost spit out the F-word, as in *fortune*."

O'Hay huffed.

Lennie said, "Did you think you might come back for it, work out the coordinates and send down a diver?"

O'Hay squinted and sniffled, scratching his bony bum by sliding on the deck.

Lennie continued, "Never fear, mate. We've got the lot, haven't we Joe? What was your plan? By the look of those ocean charts you'd marked up, and the notes in your diary, you were going to sail off to Hawaii, unload your bullion through some fellow thieves, and live the life of Riley. A very corny plan, Micky. Joe, what was the name he put in that new passport we found?"

"Adam Riley," said Joe.

"Look," said O'Hay. "We can work something out here. I still have access to a lot of money."

"Oh, Micky. You're such a smooth talker. What *are* you offering?"

"Diamonds."

"Ooh. Forever stones. So now we have an additional charge of attempting to pervert the course of justice."

O'Hay farted. "You low-lifes," he hissed. "Fucking madmen."

On the horizon, lightning flickered more brightly and thunder rumbled louder. Gusts whipped the sea into patches of foam.

"We need to wrap this up," said Joe, who pointed at the front of his T-shirt. "This bloke's on his way."

"Got you," said Lennie, who was not keen on ducking bolts thrown by the Lightning Man at sea.

O'Hay said, "What's happening?"

"You've been found guilty on all counts," Lennie said. "Now you will be sentenced."

He and Joe unroped from the foredeck the six squares of steel mesh that Joe had transported from the back garden at home. They floored one square on the deck, and wired against it two chunks of heavy-gauge railway track. They padlocked the corners of the squares until only the front piece of the cage remained to be fitted.

O'Hay's eyes bobbled and he lost control of his lower body sphincter muscles. "Guys. Guys. Let's talk. I've got millions. This is mad. I mean...I'm sorry, I didn't mean to call you ma-a..."

"Ma-a," said Joe. "Ma-a...he sounds like a sheep."

Lennie looked at the cage, then at O'Hay, then back at the cage. White light strobed above *Flamingo*.

"We need to talk," Lennie said to Joe, nodding towards the cabin.

Below deck, seated at the long table, Lennie massaged his skull. He looked through a door into the V-berth at the front of the boat:

a freshly oiled and fueled chainsaw they called Butch was sitting on a lifejacket.

"I'm having very troubling thoughts," said Lennie.

"What sort of thoughts?"

"Are we really going to chop him up and sink him in that sea basket?"

8 – A PILLAR OF SOCIETY

BACK ON DECK, Lennie studied Aunty D's and Don Gerrity's tormentor.

Lennie's revulsion was powerful for this slobbering man who listed on his accounting business website, among his many virtues and community contributions, his roles as a justice of the peace, a school board trustee, a children's football coach, and his devotion to his wife and two teenage daughters. O'Hay was even a board member of a not-for-profit aged care home. Talk about a two-faced arsehole.

Lennie scratched the nipple in the centre of his hypnotic wheel and eyed his axe before turning his gaze to Mr Lovecraft and his shiny spear. He'd already given the same orders to Butch the chainie.

"At ease, soldiers," he said.

Joe shrugged.

O'Hay appeared to sense a change in the wind on various levels and wheezed with relief. "Thank God," he said.

White light spat viciously overhead. The air shuddered; sounds like artillery fire ripped around the *Flamingo*.

Lennie looked at the accountant and his pleading, fish-like eyes, and his skin which flickered various shades of grey under the roiling sky lights.

"Why did you do it to my aunty?" said Lennie, sounding tired. "And to Don, and the others?"

"It was a mistake," said O'Hay.

"What made you realise that?" said Lennie. "At what point in your life did that fact dawn?"

O'Hay bowed his head.

Lennie said, "We're going to do you a very unusual favour. You need to think about how you can repent for the evil you've done to people."

O'Hay lifted his head. "Terrific. We can turn this into a win-win. Those diamonds are on my boat. You guys can dive, can't you? And I've got more."

"Oh, Micky," said Lennie. "Someone tipped us off about those sparklers, as well as the yellow bricks. They gave us the emails too. You know, the ones with you calling my aunty an old hag. You've made some serious enemies. Some very close to home too. Very close to home."

"What do you mean?"

"You've got to think outside the square now," said Lennie. "To keep yourself outside the cage."

"Charity work," blurted O'Hay. "I'll volunteer."

Lennie gave the accountant an eagle eye. "Yeah? Reckon you could hand out hot soup and blankets to street people at night with Joe and me? Or cold bottled water and fruit in summer?"

"Sure," said O'Hay, looking like he had cracked a winning idea and was glimpsing salvation. "I could even earn some money and pay people back, make donations, that sort of thing."

"You're a fast reformer."

"You've shown me the light today."

Joe groaned.

Lennie said, "Mm...we're all in a very difficult spot right now, Micky. Because you'd say anything to save yourself. You see, let's say we let you toddle off to do your good works. But instead, you go running to the police. You squeal like a little piggy. Ham it up a bit. We go to jail."

"You can trust me," O'Hay said.

"*How* can we trust you?"

"You could test me...set me free a little bit at a time. So I can prove myself."

"What? We let you go like a hooked fish on a loose line?" said Lennie. "Wind you back in if we don't like your direction?"

"Wow!" shouted Joe. "Check it out." He pointed at a sea snake swimming at the tail of the yacht.

"A yellow-belly," said Lennie, pondering the creature. "Can you catch it?"

"What for?" said Joe

"I've got an idea," said Lennie. "This is an omen!"

Joe shook his head. He could see Lennie was drifting into the world of Delling that blurred fact and fiction and Joe was cool with that world when you could turn it off with a switch, like a TV, or by closing a page. But he was not so cool with the idea of bringing one of the world's deadliest snakes on board in real life. His scalp burned in his Mr Darian spot.

9 – THE BEAUTY OF LIGHTNING

JOE REACHED for a long metal pole that was inserted into a plastic pipe secured to the cabin roof. The pole had a fine-mesh basket on its end. He stepped to the stern and scooped the black-and-yellow-striped creature from the sea in a single movement. The snake was not happy.

A burst of thick warm air rushed over the water. It lifted Lennie's wig off and carried it into the sky and out of sight. He was simply a man now, free of adornment. He felt lighter on a range of levels and liked it.

"Hopefully, it's just a squall," said Joe. "Not a monster settling in. Speaking of which, what am I meant to do with this thing?" The snake writhed furiously, trying to escape the basket.

"Talk to it," said Lennie, who grabbed the rope attached to the handle of the red bucket and tossed the container into the sea. He dragged it full of water and placed it slopping on the deck.

"Here's what I'm prepared to offer," Lennie said to O'Hay. "We both put our hands in this bucket. Then my friend here drops the snake in. If you keep your hand in longer than I do, or I get bitten and you don't, we set you free."

"This is insane," said O'Hay.

"If you say that one more time, I'll prove your point and stick you in that cage," said Lennie.

"Is it venomous?" said O'Hay.

"Only if it bites."

"I'm not doing it."

"I'm putting my life in the bucket with yours," said Lennie, scratching his hypnotic wheel tatt. "Or you can go straight into the sea basket, and sink and think about what might have been. For a few minutes anyway."

"O...kay," said O'Hay, whose tone suggested he had a plan.

"Good," said Lennie. "The Justice Machine can decide our fates."

O'Hay shook his head. "A snake's an animal, not a machine."

"That's your biggest problem, Micky," said Lennie. "You're a one-dimensional thinker."

"Huh?"

"A machine isn't only a bunch of nuts and bolts," Lennie explained. "It's a word for a process that transforms things."

Joe muffled a groan at the prosecutor's drift. O'Hay was a virus, plain and simple, and he'd keep destroying vulnerable people until his dying day. Joe decided on a faster path.

He knew a yellow-bellied sea snake was ten times more venomous than an Egyptian cobra. Sir David Attenborough had told him so on TV last week. Joe moved to flick the snake onto O'Hay. Lennie stepped in the way.

"You right, mate?" Lennie asked Joe. "Looks like you need a beer."

Joe turned the basket to stop the snake from jiggling out. Thunder cracked. Lightning flashed. Joe shook his head and said to Lennie, "A process that transforms things, hey? We'll all be charcoal if you don't crack on."

Lennie cut the zip-locks off O'Hay's wrists and ankles using the axe head like a knife. The inside of his skull tingled. Go with it, Lennie told himself, let's see where we land. He squatted on the deck near the bucket.

O'Hay grabbed the drink cooler and moved to sit on it.

"No. You're not resting your balls like that," said Lennie. "You squat like me, or we could be here for days."

Joe tapped a foot. "We need to put a clock on this."

"Agreed," said Lennie.

Joe was inclined to employ one of nature's timers such as a lightning flash or thunderclap as a closing bell, but the world around them was already a blistering battlefield of such effects with mere moments between bursts. He reached into his shorts pocket and pulled out O'Hay's time machine.

"Seven minutes?" he suggested, looking at the watch face, opting for an odd number that would work in Lennie's favour.

Lennie nodded.

O'Hay squinted. "What if it's a draw? You know, the snake doesn't bite anyone."

Lennie grinned. "Are you thinking the snake might get stuck in that grey area between good and evil? Limbo."

"You really think a snake's got a brain like that?" said O'Hay.

"O ye of little faith, Micky."

Joe lifted his eyebrows and looked at Lennie. "He's got a point about the draw, mate. Happens at the football, could happen here."

Lennie pondered. "OK. If Mr Yellow-belly here keeps his gun holstered, then you'll be coming to live and work with us at the Firefly Electrics Company."

O'Hay brightened. "Great. Let's forget this snake shit. I'm in. I'll be reformed in no time, promise."

"Reformation. It' not just a word, Micky. It takes commitment."

"I'll put my mind to it," O'Hay said earnestly. "I'll work hard."

"No need for you to raise a sweat on that score," Lennie said reassuringly. "If you join us at Firefly, we'd re-wire your mind as a community service, no charge, wouldn't we Joe?"

O'Hay moaned.

Joe revisited the merits of sculpting O'Hay's brain with Butch the chainsaw on the *Flamingo's* deck. He said, "Shit yeah, Mr O'Hay. You'll be a model citizen before you know it, one way or another."

O'Hay's chest deflated. He pondered his navel. The snake squirmed in the basket.

"Show time," said Lennie.

O'Hay glanced towards the seaside horizon; his eyes narrowed; his ears pricked up.

"Earth to O'Hay!" Lennie called.

O'Hay massaged his wrists and ankles and shook the muscles on his arms and legs as if he was about to go jogging. He sat on his haunches on the other side of the bucket and rubbed his palms together.

Joe looked at the men, their testicles bunched under their buttocks, shaping up to each other like underfed sumo wrestlers. This is fucking ridiculous, he thought. He made a decision.

Joe arched his back and held the pole-basket containing the snake as if he was a fisherman about to cast a rod, intending to hurl the creature back into the ocean. After that, he and Butch would get to work.

"Trust her," Lennie called to Joe as if he sensed Joe's wavering spirit. "Mother Nature can make the call here, OK?"

Shit, thought Joe, that was a nifty move by Lennie. Faith in Mother Nature was part of the Firefly Electrics Ethos. Did he believe in it, or was it just a PR stunt?

Lennie put his left hand into the bucket of water. O'Hay's eyes darted across the sea; he appeared to be listening for something.

"In!" Lennie demanded.

O'Hay immersed the fingertips of his right hand.

Joe tipped the snake gently into the bucket, fighting the urge to drop it on O'Hay's skull. It swam around the men's wrists. Then reared its head. It slid up Lennie's forearm, tongue flicking. Lennie met its black eyes with his own dark pupils. The snake fell back into the water. Seconds passed. O'Hay shuffled. His sudden movement spooked the snake, which flicked in the bucket. Both men held their hands steady. The snake lifted its head over the lip of the bucket and studied O'Hay.

Joe kept an eye on the snake and mentally practised his snake-bite first-aid routine. Pressure bandage; disable the limb; keep the victim calm; preserve the snake for the doctors.

O'Hay turned an ear to a sound in the distance, far beyond the yacht. An engine. A machine becoming louder. He ripped his hand from the bucket and plunged his entire body over the side of the *Flamingo Sky*, churning through the water in a foam of flailing arms before he tired. He trod water and waved, screaming: "Here! Help! Help!"

Lennie and Joe were trying to catch the snake, which had spilled from the overturned bucket onto the deck. It slithered and snapped. Lennie slipped bum-first onto the wet boards, swinging a foot perilously close to the snake's head before he rolled to safety. Joe flung a beach towel over the serpent and wrapped it up. He flicked it into the sea like he was doing nothing more complicated than shaking sand off the towel at the beach.

"I'll be back," said Joe, who went below. He returned seconds later carrying a hunting rifle with a telescopic sight.

"Up there," said Lennie, pointing so Joe could follow his line of sight into the sky and see the source of the engine noise.

"Help!" O'Hay yelled. "Help!"

Into the crosshairs of the gunsight, Joe put the glistening white body of a propeller-driven aircraft. The plane was swallowed by brooding clouds that were lashed with white light.

Lennie shook his head. "Stupid prick. I reckon he thought it was a boat."

The static in the air caused strands of Joe's hair to rise. He lowered the barrel, an eye still peering through the gunsight, and found O'Hay bobbing among the whitecaps, waving wildly. He unlocked the safety catch and put O'Hay's skull in the crosshairs. The *Flamingo* bucked on the swell; O'Hay's face slid in and out of the centre cross.

"We made a deal with him," said Joe, his finger closing over the trigger as a drooping moustache entered the viewfinder.

"Do we want his body floating around for people to find with a hole in its head?" said Lennie.

"If we put enough lead in 'im, he'll sink."

Lennie grinned. "Give me a sec, mate."

Joe sighed and swung the rifle to his side. Lennie unclipped a red and white lifesaver ring that was attached to the roof of the cabin beside the mainmast.

"Seriously?" said Joe.

"I was all set to waste this prick," said Lennie. "And now I'm acting like Mother Theresa. I think I need counselling."

"Fuck the counselling," said Joe, looking up. "We've got a visitor dropping in."

Black clouds swirled overhead. Darkness engulfed them as if night was coming early.

Lennie took a backswing and hurled the ring at O'Hay. It spun on the wind like a flying saucer. "Whoops!" Lennie cried as the lifesaver clunked the accountant's skull. O'Hay grabbed it and clung on.

Joe shook his head and chuckled. "Now what?"

"Oh, fuck," said Lennie, realising he'd forgotten to hold onto the rope that was attached to the ring.

Raindrops fell, hard and fat as stones. A sizzling bolt cracked into the mainmast, shattering a cup-shaped wind vane at its top. O'Hay disappeared among the boiling whitecaps.

"Let's drop another sea anchor and ride this out below," said Lennie. He leaped into the cabin and opened a locker from which he extracted a small, orange parachute that was attached to a long rope. He tossed it up the stairs to Joe. "Don't forget to tie it on!"

Flamingo's main mast swayed drunkenly, the steel rigging slapped and clanged. Joe crawled on his knees towards the bow; the deck tipped almost vertically into the trough of a foamy swell. He grabbed a tubular safety rail until the boat righted itself, and lashed the anchor rope to a bollard. He hurled the parachute into the sea, wiping spray from his eyes, making sure it inflated with water. A head-high white cap tipped its crest and smashed into the side of the boat behind Joe, surging over the deck, trying to drag him with it back into the sea. Joe was free-sliding, snatching at the railing, eyes blurry and burning with salt. He missed the rail, went over the side head-first. A monster wave smacked his face. He closed his eyes, held his breath.

He threw up a leg, feeling his shin shear along the steel-wire safety rails. His ankle burned. Something had locked onto his foot. He kicked. It wouldn't let go. He trusted the grip on his foot, reached up – and grabbed a railing post.

Lennie, with a rope around his waist and lying on the foredeck, had Joe's ankle clamped in a double-handed grip. *Flamingo* bounced like a bronco trying to toss her riders. Joe tugged on the post and hauled himself back on deck. Pounded by water, Lennie guided them toward the cabin by pulling on his waist-rope that was secured to a bollard.

With the hatch sealed and bolted, they turned their attention to Joe's shin. The skin was scarlet from the kneecap to the ankle after being dragged along the steel wire. But it wasn't bleeding.

"You sure that's a real leg?" asked Lennie. "A normal person's would be stripped to the bone."

"Works for me," said Joe. "Though I could use a pain killer while we ride this out."

Flamingo bucked and its joints creaked. Her crew sipped beers and looked through opposite portholes at the storm – Lennie to starboard, Joe to port. They both heard the same eye-popping *ka-thack!* Lennie missed most of the accompanying blaze of light on Joe's side that speared into the sea.

The electric blade cut one of O'Hay's arms from his body; Joe glimpsed the pink and black limb floating away from the accountant's head and shoulders. A cresting wave interrupted his view. Inside the next trough, Joe saw O'Hay's face; his eyes appeared to be open and looking at Joe. Joe waved. O'Hay submerged as if something was pulling his body down. Joe watched in silence.

"Can you see him?" said Lennie.

"Nup," said Joe, who stared at the empty lifesaver ring bobbing in the whitewater.

• • • •

THE BLACK SKY WAS SHOWING the sailors its back and heading east. A shallow mist sat upon the sea, speared here and there by sunlight through holes in grey clouds.

Back on deck, Lennie said, "We should search for him."

"OK," said Joe, pointing the rifle's telescope in the opposite direction to where he saw O'Hay electrocuted.

"Can you see him?" said Lennie, who moved to press the starter button on the yacht's engine, but he was distracted by a mechanical throbbing inside the murk. "Hear that?"

Joe aimed the telescope into the mist. "We've got a problem."

In the crosshairs of the magnified circle, the hazy, brown hulk of a ship was growing large. Filthy smoke spewed from its funnel.

"Let me see," said Lennie, taking the rifle from Joe and peering into the scope. "Jesus Christ! It's the *Lord!* She's gonna cut us in half!"

He tossed the rifle to Joe and pressed the ignition button on the inboard engine. It coughed with a nasty bronchial rattle and died.

Joe raised his eyebrows. "I told you to change those sparkplugs."

The engine coughed uselessly again.

Lennie was struck by the possibility that Trixie Talaveda and the Enoka brothers had traded him and Joe to the drug dealers and terrorists who lost their cash from the *Lord of Saigon*. Had they triangulated this point in the ocean via the signal on his phone, which was now pulsing on the table in the cabin below, and sent their ship to track the *Flamingo* and destroy them?

It was as if Father Francesco had risen from the sea trench underneath them and was striking Lennie's boy-body with vicious blows. Lennie's nostrils filled with the boiled-cabbage body odour and sewer breath of the men who had shuffled into his Sunday school tents. He instinctively reached for a Jack, but he was naked. The world around him moved in slow motion and his body went numb; he could move neither fingers nor limbs.

Joe emerged from the cabin holding a flare gun. He fired. A tracer of violet light soared into the sky; its cap exploded, spraying purple tentacles that wafted through the heavens like a luminous jellyfish.

The ship blew its horn, its scabbed hull scraped *Flamingo* and sent her yawing to one side, then reeling like a hit and groggy boxer. The yacht soon did what it does best and steadied on its lead-weighted keel.

Lennie and Joe watched the stern of the ship shrinking into the fog.

Feeling seeped back into Lennie's limbs. Had he just tasted the state of mind the doctors had red-flagged?

"That wasn't the *Lord*," said Joe. "It was just some Russian rust bucket."

"How do you know that?"

"The flag, mate," Joe lied, for he had actually read the vessel's name, *Admiral Vladivostok*. "I know the flag from Vlad. You know, the bloke from Moscow who drinks at the Rose & Thistle."

Lennie was in no mood to press the point. "Do you reckon he's still alive?"

Joe decided not to tell Lennie what he saw through the porthole. He said nothing because Lennie's light changed the moment he threw the lifesaver to O'Hay. There had emerged on Lennie's face a glow that Joe hadn't seen for a long time. It was the face of the destined-to-lose footy fans on the TV replays when they still had hope. Yeah, *hope* was the word, thought Joe. What was it

Lennie had told O'Hay? *It's fundamental to existence, hope...take it away and a lot of people lose the will to live.*

Joe wanted Lennie to have it for as long as he could make it last.

Joe said, "Maybe the Russians will pick him up."

Lennie rubbed his chin. "It's a possibility, I guess. But there's a certainty too."

"What's that?" said Joe.

Lennie smiled. "The Justice Machine will decide his fate."

Joe raised his eyebrows. "I was going to ask you about that."

"Popped into my head while I was looking at O'Hay."

"A process that transforms things, hey? You've been reading too many books, mate. Scumbags like O'Hay should go straight into a meat grinder. Or Butch could have done the job like we planned."

Lennie scratched his buttock. "Do you know who's in charge of that machine?"

"Ah, so it's got a boss, hey?" Joe scanned the sea. The clouds were giving way to blue sky and sunlight.

"Mother Nature."

"Phew, this is getting deep."

"We humans are Mother Nature's biggest problem."

"Filthy bastards," growled Joe, who used the pole basket to scoop a floating yellow box labelled *medical waste* out of the water. "So what do we do about it?"

"Follow the Firefly Ethos, mate."

Joe nodded. "Isn't there a word for people like O'Hay who won't stop being arseholes?"

"Recidivists."

"Sounds religious. Some sort of cult."

Lennie grumbled. "Don't get me going." But his mind was already going, thinking about how the legal system had protected so-called *Pillars of Society* like O'Hay, Darian, and Francesco. His limbs started to feel numb again.

"Listen, mate," said Joe, scooping up a plastic bottle to return to Halcion Bay for recycling. "We can't just sit on our arses complaining to the wall when bad people get away with bad stuff."

• • • •

UNDER THE LIFTING FOG, the surface of the sea emerged with a mirror shine. They washed the material evidence of O'Hay's existence off the *Flamingo* with saltwater using a high-pressure pump and hose.

Then they bathed naked at the side of the yacht, washing themselves sparkling clean before drying with towels on the wooden deck and warming their bodies under the midday sun.

They opened cold beers and fished with handlines before heading home with a feed of pink snapper in the red bucket.

After mooring the *Flamingo*, they gutted the fish at the beach beside the jetty and fed seagulls with the scraps. Joe parcelled a handful of fillets in cling film, they give them to a scrawny, sleepy-looking boy who was watching them, sitting on his bicycle.

"For ya mum," said Joe.

"She's dead," said the boy.

"Give 'em to your dad," said Joe.

"I'll cook 'em," said the boy, unslinging a backpack to put the fish inside.

Lennie and Joe turned and walked towards the Firefly.

Lennie whispered to Joe, "That kid's bike. It's the one we saw against the toilet block when we loaded up this morning."

"Noticed that," said Joe, scratching his forehead. "Potential witness, hey?"

"Tricky," said Lennie.

"Hang on," the boy called, riding towards them. He took his backpack off and reached inside. "This yours?"

The boy was holding a camel-coloured slip-on shoe with leather tassels. "I saw you guys on the jetty, getting into your dinghy. It dropped from that thing you were carrying."

"Thanks, mate," said Joe, taking O'Hay's missing shoe. He winked at the kid. "Panfried is best."

"I don't eat shoes," said the kid.

"You're smarter than you look," said Joe, who gave the smiling youth a high-five.

Before leaving Halcion Bay, they separated O'Hay's clothes and footwear into three plastic bags. On the fringes of the city, they stopped at three different street-side rubbish bins in different suburbs and dumped the bags.

At home that night, they ate pan-fried snapper and hand-cut chips while drinking beer and sitting on the sofa in the lounge room with Rawcus – who hated fish but liked chips. They were joined by Bruce the cat, who although deaf and one-eyed had a great nose for raw snapper which he chewed off a plate on the floor.

"This is the life," Joe said, putting his feet on the coffee table while they watched a British TV crime series called *Luther*.

"You wouldn't want a bloke like him on your case," said Joe, as Detective Chief Inspector Luther reconstructed a villain's cheekbones with his knuckles.

"It's fiction, mate," said Lennie. "Real plods aren't that good." Lennie hoped that was true.

"Fiction, hey," said Joe, eyeing the DVD stack by the telly. "Pulp next, yeah?"

Oh, Gawd, thought Lennie, I'm jack of Tarantino. But what are friends for? "Sure, mate."

Rawcus patrolled the back edge of the sofa making wah-wah noises, bowing now and then to show off his sulphur crest.

"Can't you come up with a different tune, cobber?" said Lennie, who was hearing the bird's cries as police sirens and wondering where O'Hay was.

Joe couldn't bear to see the furrows etching themselves into Lennie's brow. Hope's light was fading from his friend's face. Joe spilled the beans on O'Hay's lightning strike.

Rawcus swallowed a chip and tongued his beak clean, striding the sofa back. He chirped, "In the end, mate...in the end, mate...the bloke got the exit he deserved."

Lennie and Joe looked at each other in amazement. Rawcus had perfectly quoted Bullseye Donovan who had waxed lyrical at the Rose & Thistle when a politician who frequented the pub escaped jail on a charge of sexually assaulting a minor, who committed suicide during the trial. The polly, after celebrating, crashed his car into a power pole. When he rolled out of his door, he was electrocuted by a live wire carrying 22,000 volts.

Lennie looked the bird in the eye. "Rawcus, what goes on in that brain of yours?"

"You talkin' to me?" the bird replied, foreshadowing another Bullseye favourite.

"It's all in the mind, isn't it?" said Lennie.

"The mind's a fuckin' mystery, mate," said Rawcus. "Big as the universe."

10 – MOPPING UP

ENNIE'S new phone bleated with the sound of sheep. He turned away from his view through the windscreen of the Firefly which was parked beside a city cemetery on a headland overlooking the sapphire blue Pacific Ocean under midday sun.

The call was arriving via WhatsApp and fully encrypted, he hoped.

"Is it her?" said Joe.

"Knock, knock," chimed Rawcus, who was patrolling on Joe's shoulder. "Who's there?"

"No-one else has the number," said Lennie. "Not from us, anyway."

Lennie, wearing latex gloves, tapped the handset to switch on the open speaker and answered, "This is Barry."

A female voice said, "I just had a second visit from the police."

"They suspicious?"

"I don't think so. Not of me. They gave me an update on the search..."

The caller explained that O'Hay's work colleagues had contacted her too, and they had also made a report to the police when the boss failed to come to work two days in a row and didn't answer his phone.

She added that the police had discovered O'Hay's car abandoned near the inner-city marina where he had berthed his now missing boat.

Lennie said, "Do they have any leads on what happened to the boat?"

"They were of the view that Michael sailed it out himself secretly at night."

"They may be spinning a web for us," said Lennie. "Did you ask if the security cameras at the marina could shed any light?"

"They saw nothing because they were focused on the footpaths and jetties. Very poor security, the police said."

"Ah, never fear," said Lennie. "No doubt the marina will lift its game now the horse has bolted."

Rawcus bobbed and squawked. "And the field is away for race nine at Randwick...!"

Joe grabbed Rawcus's beak. The bird went the bite on his fingers.

"Who was that?" said the caller.

"Sorry," said Lennie, rolling his eyes at Joe and Rawcus. "We were listening to the races on the radio."

Joe grabbed Rawcus by the legs and opened the door to step outside.

"Murder!" cried Rawcus, as Joe threw the door shut and stepped towards the cemetery gates.

"Sorry," said Lennie. "Have you done the other things on the list?"

"Yes."

"Did you ever give him an engraved Rolex?"

"Never. Why?"

"Nothing important," said Lennie. "I'll be in touch."

· · · ·

LENNIE MADE A CALL to Tom Steele, Crime Editor of the *City Daily*.

Steele said, "I think I recognise your voice, pal. Mr Wharf?"

"You must be dreaming, Tom-Tom," said Lennie. "But I do have a tip for a jungle drummer like you."

"What's your name?" said Steele.

"Psychology Jones," said Lennie, choosing the name of an African dictator from Angola who struck Lennie as a deep thinker worthy of imitation.

Lennie and Steele chatted.

Lennie stepped out of the Firefly and waited. The sun was warm. He heard a machine approaching – and lobbed his handset into the back jaws and grinding teeth of a passing rubbish truck.

"Sneaky bastard!" screeched Rawcus from atop his mobile perch on Joe's shoulder as the subservient redhead beneath his claws trudged from the cemetery gates towards Lennie.

"Beer o'clock, mates?" the bird suggested.

• • • •

THE NEXT DAY, A STORY appeared in the *City Daily* by Tom Steele, quoting "a friend of the colourful financial adviser, Michael O'Hay" who said he had "done a runner" to another part of the world after stealing millions from his clients that he had converted into cash, gold, and diamonds.

Hawaii by boat, and then to South America by air, was the most likely plan. The claims of the anonymous friend were supported by the police who had discovered O'Hay had booked airline tickets to take him from Honolulu to Rio de Janeiro. The authorities figured he was well away from Sydney and deep into the South Pacific where he may be in hiding on any number of islands aboard his yacht, *Make Hay,* aiming to sell or dump the vessel and fly into a new life with a new identity.

• • • •

12 MONTHS LATER.

No trace of the gold, diamonds, yacht, or O'Hay had been found.

Lennie, Joe, and Rawcus were driving from their home to visit Aunty Doreen's grave at the Pinegrove Memorial Park on the third anniversary of her passing. They had a detour to make along the way.

Inside the van, Rawcus went nuts in the back trying to find the quiz drawer containing the pumpkin seeds. Lennie read on his phone to Joe an online news story written by Steele about the coroner's findings in the deaths of two men.

Jona and Toku Enoka, the coroner concluded, had died from "misadventure".

"Miss Adventure," said Joe, his brow wrinkling. "She's quite dangerous, then?"

"You idiot!" Rawcus screeched, tossing around drawers.

Lennie read on. As the coroner told it, the Enoka brothers were alone aboard a stolen four-wheel-drive in remote bushland while on the run from the Australian Federal Police, who were hunting them for an alleged terrorist plot, when they stopped to shoot ducks in a dam.

It was high summer, so they were wearing shorts, and rubber flip-flops on their feet. A snake had bitten Jona on the calf and, in a panic to shoot the snake with a shotgun, he had blasted Toku in the head. A shocked Jona had died of a cardiac arrest, triggered by brown snake toxin and exacerbated by his own fat-clogged arteries, on the edge of the dam, where he fell by Toku's face-shredded body. Jona had been wearing an expensive Swiss watch engraved on its back with the words: *To Michael. Love Always, Possum.* The investigating police had no explanation for the source of the mysterious watch, other than to speculate that the Enokas had been mugging people. If no-one claimed it, the watch would be auctioned and the proceeds would go into the State's coffers.

"Mate," said Lennie, rubbing his chin. "We'd be sleeping better if we knew Pago, and Chris and John were in the same boat as their big bro's, hey."

"Two down is better than none," said Joe, who wasn't afraid of the surviving Enoka brothers but would have preferred a world without them.

"Shit!" said Lennie. "This other yarn by our new journo mate might explain the lack of a certain visitor in our lives since we put that Rolex to work in the tax pack.

"Trixie Talaveda?" guessed Joe.

"Bingo!" cried Rawcus, who'd finally found the drawer of seeds.

"You lunatic," Lennie called over his shoulder to the bird. He turned back to his phone screen. "Tom-Tom says she's the subject of a *missing person* report."

Steele's article said that the authorities suspected the Enokas, who were known to associate with Trixie, may have killed her and hidden the body in the bush while on the run.

"That's sad news," said Joe. "The makings of a mystery."

What Lennie didn't mention to Joe as he read was that he had unravelled another mystery: he knew about Joe's adult literacy classes.

A few weeks ago, he had opened Joe's post, as he routinely did, only passing on to him the important stuff. Joe had achieved a "highly commended" in his most recent semester. Lennie was pleased as punch for Joe. Because what would happen to Joe, and

Rawcus, if Lennie died and Joe still couldn't read? Lennie had decided to say diddly-squat unless Joe chose to go there, at which point he would simply express warm surprise at his friend's initiative and achievement.

Lennie's regular phone rang with the theme tune of the old *Twilight Zone* TV show. No Caller ID showed on his screen. Fuck it, thought Lennie, he was feeling lucky. "Firefly Electrics. Lennie speaking."

"Hello," said a young voice. "Is that Mr Larson?"

"How can I help?"

"I met you and your friend last year at Halcion Bay. You gave me some fish."

Lennie motioned at Joe, who glanced at him. Lennie whispered, "The kid who found the shoe."

"Good to hear from you," Lennie said into the phone. "How'd you find me?"

"You've heard of the internet, Mr Larson?"

Lennie rolled his eyes at Joe. "You looking to get your lights fixed, are you?"

"Na. But I found something else that belongs to you."

"Oh."

"Yeah. A foam ring washed up on the beach with the name of your boat on it. *Flamingo Sky*. I thought you might want it back."

"What's your name?"

"Smiley."

"Tell you what, Smiley. You hang on to it. And next time we're down at the bay, we'll get in touch. Maybe you'd like to come fishing?"

"Are you guys pedo's?"

"You got a radar for that sort of stuff?"

"I guess I'll find out."

• • • •

"WHAT NUMBER IS IT?" asked Joe, parking in front of a three-storey brick box of apartments a few suburbs short of the cemetery. Some innovative souls had ripped the seats out of a car that was propped up curbside on a stack of bricks instead of wheels. The innovators had arranged the seats in a row along the front wall of the building where tattooed, glassy-eyed young men and women sat and scratched in the mid-morning sun.

"Must be that one there," said Lennie, pointing at a ground-floor apartment with a wheelchair access ramp leading from the footpath to the front door.

Minutes later, they were sitting at a plastic kitchen table inside the government-owned flat sipping hot, milky tea and passing a smoking joint to a wheelchair-bound woman with straw-coloured, shoulder-length hair; clear milk-coloured skin; and large eyes with sea-green irises.

Joe, with Rawcus standing politely on his shoulder, fondled a sporting trophy he had plucked off a shelf on the wall by the table. It was a miniature lawn bowl, about the size of a billiard ball, which was mounted on a block of polished wood. An engraved plaque was screwed into the base. Joe read the words under his breath, trying not to move his lips: *Doreen Dixon and Don Gerrity, Mixed Doubles Champions. Erskineville Lawn Bowling Club. Seniors Division.*

"I might take up bowls," said Joe.

Rawcus bobbed. "Head like a bowling ball, this kid...thick as a brick!"

Lennie said, "Aunty D's bowls are in the cupboard at home. I'll dig 'em out later, and we can give 'em a shot on the hallway rug."

"You'd prefer grass over carpet, wouldn't you, Joe," said Pauline, grinning, exhaling a small cloud before handing the joint to Joe.

Pauline Gerrity became a paraplegic after being knocked off her motor scooter by a truck the year after she left high school, where Joe and Lennie completed a brief stint in the junior years, as required by the laws of the State.

Pauline eyed a box that Lennie had placed on her kitchen table. The box was wrapped in candy-striped paper and tied with a blue ribbon that was frayed and scraggly at one end.

"Rawcus insisted on helping Joe with the ribbon," said Lennie, who sipped his tea, trying to look like he was enjoying it. He hated powdered milk.

"My birthday's not until next week," she said.

"Best you open it now," said Lennie. "So there's no confusion when you do."

"No confusion!" said Rawcus.

Pauline slid the ribbon off the box and opened it. She was puzzled when she pulled out a wad of used Australian banknotes from dozens of bundles packed tightly inside.

"My God," she said. "What's this for?"

"A present from your dad," said Lennie.

Pauline gawped, speechless.

"He left it for you with friends of my Aunty Doreen for safekeeping. It has just matured."

"What friends?" she said, eyebrows raised.

"They'd prefer to remain anonymous."

"Would they now?"

"Yes, they're quite shy. Aren't they, Joe?"

Joe stared into his teacup. "Don't put that stuff in the bank, Pauls."

"Bugger the banks!" said Rawcus, doing his best Bullseye Donovan impression. "Bloody robbers, they are!"

Pauline smiled and cocked an eye at Lennie. She waited silently.

"You don't want the bloody tax man hoovering it up," said Lennie. "Best to dribble it out here and there. We'll finish that floor safe in your bedroom now, but we'll have to come back next week to fix the lights in the bathroom. We have another appointment today we can't miss."

Lennie's phone rang. Rawcus tried to whistle along with the *Twilight Zone* tune. The humans grimaced.

Lennie let it ring out. "Just a client. We've got a meeting soon."

"That was wonderful, Rawcus," said Pauline.

Encouraged, the bird tried again with the same effect on his audience.

• • • •

JOE SAID TO RAWCUS, "We need you to stay in the Firefly, mate. Yell if there's trouble. OK?"

Rawcus sulked in the back of the van.

Lennie and Joe stepped through the cemetery gates. Joe wheeled beside him a compact travel case with a telescopic handle. They placed a bunch of flowers on the memorial to the nurse Jacinta Turner. Then walked to Aunty D's grave.

A slightly-built woman stepped from under the branches of a tree. She was wearing a sleeveless, floral-patterned summer dress. Her dark hair was cut into a bob that partly shaded her eyes. Her black shoes were flat-heeled and she wore little make-up. She stood next to Lennie and Joe.

The woman placed a large bunch of flowers on Aunty D's grave. "Sorry," was all she had written on the note attached to the flowers. No name. And she didn't say a word to Lennie and Joe as she stood beside them. Neither did the boys say a word to Michael O'Hay's wife.

Joe parked the wheelie case and peeled off his hands a pair of flesh-coloured latex gloves.

Lennie and Joe walk away empty-handed.

Cheryl O'Hay grasped the handle of the case and pulled it awkwardly along the footpath to a different car park. Its contents were heavy. Scouting the car park to ensure she was alone, she loaded the gift-wrapped bricks one by one into the boot of her vehicle.

Behind the driver's wheel, Cheryl checked the crumpled business card for Firefly Electrics that she kept in her purse.

There was a word that Cheryl searched for in her mind as she started her car. Serendipity? Yes, that was it: *a happy chance*. It's the very word she thought of when she found that Firefly card in her letterbox a couple of years ago, with a quaint *Ethos* printed on its back. It was one of those direct-marketing drops that tradesmen did, trying to drum up business. She had phoned them about getting motion-activated security lights installed on her front porch. After the job was done, they got to talking over a cup of tea and cake. They discovered things in common, including a husband and an aunty.

She was in for a busy night. She had to deliver some early Christmas gifts of yellow metal, with all their identifying marks filed off, to a list of her missing husband's neediest clients. It helped that she had access to his office records for names and addresses, emails and suchlike.

This would be a job best done in the dark, wearing a hat and gloves, without knocking on doors, parking in backstreets distant from her targets. She liked driving the quiet roads alone in the early hours, after finishing her nursing-home nightshifts.

• • • •

THE FIREFLY LEFT THE cemetery at a sedate pace.

"Giss a kiss, love. Giss a kiss, love," squawked Rawcus as he jumped onto his pole between the front seats. Joe pushed the *ABBA Classics* CD into the player and cranked up the volume. Lennie reached into his jeans pocket and touched a Jack as they blended into the streaming traffic heading for Halcion Bay and a fishing trip with a kid named Smiley.

The End...for now

Thank you for reading *Justice Machine*, Book 1 in the *Firefly Electrics Series*.

Book 2, *Kangaroo Court*, and Book 3, *Galaxy Motel*, are available now. The opening to *Kangaroo Court* is included on the following pages.

Book 4, *Gumleaf Mafia* is coming soon.

You can get the Firefly Electrics Series boxset of Books 1-3 as an e-book at a bonus discount to the individual books.

Learn more, find more books, or join the Mark Furness Readers Club to get free books by visiting his website:

www.markfurnesswriter.com[1]

---

1.   http://www.markfurnesswriter.com

About Kangaroo Court:

Lennie, Joe, and Rawcus are touring inside a mountain forest when they discover an abandoned campervan – and a pair of stringless tennis racquets. Who would own such objects, and why?

The deeper into the forest they venture, the more mysterious things they find. They're soon headlong on a mission to save strangers from a terrifying ordeal among the trees.

Meanwhile, their partner in a secret botanical business is abducted, forcing Lennie and Joe to confront demons from their past. Can they save the childlike young man they call The Chemist?

If that's not enough to juggle, their friend Pauline Gerrity rings an alarm from her refuge for abused women and children. Her call leads Lennie and Joe to create an animated sculpture they title *Cocoon of Man* and hang anonymously from an inner-city tree. A leading art critic likens their work to the British street artist, Banksy. But when the critic adds that the mysterious tree-hangers must be "borderline psychos", Lennie and Joe aren't sure whether to be flattered or insulted.

• • • •

Part 1
ETHER

1 – DRESS CODE

A WOMAN'S DRESS billowed as if a ghost was wearing it. The red and yellow costume waltzed above a dirt road inside a tall forest on a hazy afternoon. There was a human witness.

Joe, at the wheel of the rumbling Firefly Electrics van, went drop-jawed.

Lennie dozed in the bucket seat beside him. Rawcus, perched on a wooden rod fixed between the headrests of the seats, missed the show too because a black beanie covered his feathered head.

Joe slammed his foot on the brake, throwing Lennie forward and clunking his freshly-shaven skull against the windscreen. Rawcus sensed the fast-changing momentum but couldn't stop swinging over to upside down. "Faark!" the cockatoo cried as his sleeping hood fell off.

"Sorry," said Joe, who opened his door and stepped barefoot towards a thorny, trackside shrub upon which the hibiscus-print frock had settled.

Aaaa!

At the childlike cry, Joe did a 360-degree turn, scanning patchy bush between the trunks of ancient gumtrees that squeezed both sides of the track. He could see neither man nor beast.

Lennie appeared beside him, rubbing a plum-coloured lump that was growing on his forehead. "Pig hunters?"

"Could be a pig," agreed Joe, who knew a cornered feral swine could howl like a child in pain, especially if it had a hunting dog's teeth clamped to its bum, which happened occasionally out here. "But I doubt it was wearing that," he said, nodding at the frock.

"We've seen stranger things," said Lennie, recalling a two-headed black snake he'd observed in the forest a few weeks ago. One head had been drinking from a puddle, the other head was keeping a lookout for trouble, though in hindsight Lennie conceded that a five-star hangover may have triggered double vision.

Joe peeled the short-sleeved dress off the shrub and held it up by the shoulders with banana-fingered hands that rendered the clothing doll-like in scale. The dress had a button-up front and was ripped down the back from the collar to the waist. "Someone was in a hurry to get this off."

"Passion?" Lennie suggested, entertaining optimism. He put his unusually rosy perspective down to the disorienting clunk of his head on the windscreen.

"Or the opposite," said Joe. "The wearer's not here to say."

"Jury's out then," said Lennie, who squatted and peered at tyre prints on the track. "Two vehicles," he concluded, fingering dirt then pointing. "Heading in that direction by the look of the spray. Fresh too."

Joe grinned. *By the look of the spray.* Lennie usually said this when he picked the wind direction while they sailed their little yacht, *Flamingo Sky,* on the open ocean. In a day or two, when their current mission was completed, Joe hoped once again to be whale watching from its deck at dawn. Right now, he sniffed a spanner falling into those works, but it was too early to tell how big, small, or stinky the spanner might be. The vehicle tracks turned left a couple of stone throws away, heading into a firebreak trail carved by an earthmover. The bush was making a comeback.

Joe started to retrace his steps to the van, intending to follow the tracks on wheels rather than by foot – not because he was shoeless but because they had precious cargo on board the Firefly that shouldn't be left alone, as well as Rawcus who would get inconsolably cranky if he was left behind when adventure lay ahead.

"What the hell?" barked Joe, sidestepping something dark and furry that was sliding along the gutter of the track.

If the hat-sized thing was alive, it didn't look like any creature that Joe had ever seen, even when he'd been on mind-altering adventures with Lennie, which was quite often. He thought that maybe last night's magic mushroom casserole with lamb shanks and sweet potato was staging a comeback. The blue-capped fungi had been packed with more surprises than a sack of firecrackers tossed into a campfire, which was one of Lennie's favourite party tricks and was on the menu for later tonight – if they could get to where they wanted to be.

Right now, however, Joe felt it wise to put a middleman between him and the 'thing' until its nature was known. He picked up a stick and poked it. It stopped. He lifted it into the air.

"Creepy," observed Lennie, who wasn't talking about the small, horny-backed lizard which scurried away after being revealed as the carrier of the miniature fur coat.

Joe examined his catch. "If it had blood on it, I'd swear there's been a scalping."

A red-back spider crawled from inside the wig of apparently human hair, making its way in an irritated manner along the stick towards Joe's hand. Joe watched the venomous creature step onto the back of his hand. The spider appeared to be juggling whether to run or fight. It bared its fangs.

"Help yourself," invited Joe. "But why waste your energy, buddy?"

Lennie shook his head, partly in admiration, partly in everlasting amazement, because Joe was immune to most types of spider bites. Doctors had done tests on him, but there was no chemical reason they could pin it down to. Joe reckoned he was bitten by different spiders so many times as a kid that the pain had been reduced to a feeling that was no worse than a mozzie bite. But Lennie knew that in Joe's mind, *spiders* could take many forms. Years ago, then schoolboy Joe, who was delirious during a bout of measles, told a GP that he had been bitten by a poisonous spider named Mr Darian, who was also Joe's headmaster. Boy, did the brown stuff hit the fan after that slant was put on matters?

Lennie got dragged into it by trying to cover up what Joe meant, fearing Mr Darian would twist the facts, which he did, of course. Mr Darian didn't get to be the master of 11-year-old kids like Lennie and Joe by being stupid, the boys learned. A couple of policemen talked to them, then delivered the boys to a team of smiling doctors at The Brain & Mind Institute.

The medicos' amazing brains didn't know what to make of Joe's wide definition of a spider and his claims that Mr Darian had bitten him, apart from asking sneaky questions and giving them inkblot tests. After that, the boys were filled with drugs that made them sleep for days on end.

Lennie and Joe could have done that deep-sleep shit at home in much greater comfort, they agreed later. So they hadn't spoken to any doctors since, not about brain health anyway. Doctors, they decided, were only good for fixing broken bones and stitching cuts. Lennie and Joe had decided to care for each other's brains instead, and so far it had worked out pretty well by their measure.

In the forest, Joe crouched and gently blew the spider from his hand into a pile of leaf litter. "This is shaping as a fair mystery," he said rising, holding the red and yellow dress in one hand and the black-haired wig in his other as if weighing possibilities.

"Cast-offs from a small, bald nudist?" offered Lennie.

Nie! Nie!

These screams caused Rawcus to wobble upon the rod in the van to which he had just returned using skilled but undignified wing work. Putting the sleeping beanie over his head unassisted was a trick he was yet to master. He dropped it, turning a blue-ringed black eye to the bush.

Nie!

"*That* was human," said Joe.

Lennie nodded.

The two men jumped into the van and Joe tossed the wig and dress into the back.

"Hang on," Joe warned as he sparked the ignition and floored the accelerator. Rawcus rolled backward like a gymnast on a crossbar with a casual approach to training. Joe well knew that Rawcus was mostly good-humoured if given fair notice that life was about to get bumpy, and bumpy it got.

"Hoo-roo!" cried Rawcus. "Woo-ha!"

The van leaped and fishtailed as Joe gunned off the main track and down the potholed fire trail. He spotted a parked campervan, painted with psychedelic stripes that reminded him of a rainbow Zebra he'd been reading about in a picture book for his adult literacy class homework. The back doors of the campervan were open, clothes and bedding and kitchen utensils were strewn upon the track.

Joe stopped behind the camper. "Looks like a bushwhacking," he said, combing his freckled fingers through his mop of red hair. They got stuck in the tangles. He cut the engine.

Lennie stroked the bruise on his temple as if it might be a sign of more sinister things to come. Hopefully not a tumour, he thought.

He and Joe slipped from either side of their mothership, landed on the soft earth, and looked and listened. Apart from a breeze rustling leaves, there was silence.

"Something's freaked out the locals," Joe whispered.

Lennie nodded. The absence of tweets, shrieks, and coos created a feeling at the nape of Lennie's neck like ants were crawling under his skin and nibbling his spinal cord. He massaged his vertebrae to squash the ants, taking no chances that they were real or imagined, and took a few steps forward, whereupon he squatted to examine the debris scattered behind the camper. The oddest things were two tennis racquets – with stringless heads.

Joe walked to the front of the camper. "Hey," he hissed backward at Lennie. "We have company."

"What company?"

"Police."

2 – THE BUSH WHISPERER

LENNIE WASN'T INCLINED to ask further questions. He was thinking about the home-grown marijuana they called Mars Grass that was sitting in a backpack in their van. He tiptoed backward, keeping whoever was in front of the psychedelic camper out of his line of sight so that he stayed out of theirs. He quietly opened the sliding side-door of the Firefly.

Rawcus eyed Lennie, who crossed a finger over his lips to urge the bird to maintain operational silence. Rawcus winked as if he got the message, although Lennie sometimes wondered if the bird simply had a nervous tic and in reality had no idea what Lennie was on about.

"Stay alert but not alarmed," Lennie whispered. Rawcus winked.

Lennie grabbed the backpack and pulled a throwing tomahawk from under the passenger's seat. Police officers could get pesky about drugs and weapons being carried in cars. Lennie pulled the sliding door quietly closed and backed into the undergrowth carrying his cargo, glad he was wearing jeans and heavy boots because snakes were plentiful on the forest floor in summer, and they liked to roam on hot, late afternoons like this. Some of the bastards even crawled in the overhead branches, occasionally hanging disguised like ribbons of bark. He heard a stranger's voice...

"We had a call-out to a burglary at a farm on Diamondback Road," the male said. "What's your excuse?"

"Sunday drive," replied Joe.

"It's Monday."

"Lost track of time."

"Anyone with you?"

"Not unless you count a cockatoo."

"Well, there's nothing here for you then. We have this in hand."

"We?" said Joe, raising his eyebrows.

"My partner's doing business in the bush."

Lennie's pulse kicked. He turned slowly, looking out for a squatting copper with his pants around his ankles, or a standing lawman clutching his dick. Nothing.

Lennie crab-walked, careful not to step on crisp sticks. He stopped behind a bush through which he saw the outline of the copper Joe was talking to. The forest behind him crackled and a thudding beat pressed in. He dropped the backpack and grasped the wooden handle of his tomahawk, swivelling to confront the attacker...

"What the fuck?" yelled the copper, who pulled his gun and aimed at the fast-approaching intruders.

A grey kangaroo as tall as a man bounced past Lennie and across the track near Joe and the copper, followed by two smaller bounders who, when they saw the humans, hit the panic button and crashed left and right into the scrub.

Lennie used the commotion to virtually step inside the thickly-leaved shrub beside him, a position from which he got a clearer view of the copper: he observed a fit-looking bloke in his mid-twenties, he guessed. The lawman was wearing a constable's light blue shirt and dark trousers, and was regulation-equipped: his utility belt carried a Taser, handcuffs, and a telescoping baton.

Joe said to the shaking copper, "New to the bush, are you mate?"

The sweaty-browed lawman reholstered his fat, black handgun and said to Joe, "How about you bugger off and have a good day?"

Joe turned toward the Firefly and began walking – on the spot. He was rubbish at the moonwalk, but he hoped his variation on the theme might do the trick. The copper headed in the opposite direction with quick steps. Joe ambled to the side of Lennie's shrub and pushed his shorts down. He looked at his manhood which had a helmet tattooed Hindu blue and spotted with yellow dots. Ah, the crazy things you do on your eighteenth birthday, thought Joe, who was glad he was now 33 and past his toadstool phase. Joe let it flow...

"Hoy!" hissed the bush. "I'm not waterproof."

"Sorry," said Joe, redirecting a stream fat enough to make a horse jealous. He spoke softly to the leaves: "There's a single paddy wagon up ahead. I saw it rocking."

"So you reckon they've got the owner of the wig and dress in there?"

Joe nodded. "I saw a red sandal on the track. Like my sister wore."

"You feeling heroic?" said the bush.

"Does the Phantom wear purple tights?" Joe replied, thinking about the cockroach-infested comics his dead dad left him, along with a damaged eardrum from childhood slaps that had been almost as regular as his heartbeat at times. The relevant ear itched, so he scratched it.

The bush whispered, "I'll stay here. You drive out to the main track. Then park and circle back through the bush on foot. And put some boots on!"

"Hey!" the copper called. He was standing back by the front of the Firefly. "What's with the bush whisperer act?"

"I have a brain condition," said Joe, who shook his hose and pulled up his shorts. "It makes me talk to trees with my dick in my hands. A type of Curette Syndrome, apparently."

"I think you mean Tourette," said the copper, who put his hands on his hips, drawing attention to the assorted artillery on his belt. "You've got two choices, smartarse. Hit the road, or I'll strip search you and your vehicle."

"I'll pick number one, thanks," said Joe, who was tempted by number two and smiled, wondering if the copper liked toadstools.

"Last warning, blockhead," growled the copper.

Joe put his hands up in mock surrender and climbed into the van, pulling his door shut. Before he could hit the ignition, a nerve-jangling cry echoed through his open window. Then a yelp, quickly muffled. The sounds came from the direction of the paddy wagon. Joe heard the crisp tap of metal-upon-metal and turned: the nose of the copper's gun was poking into his window and aimed at his head.

The copper said, "Step out of the vehicle. Don't be a hero."

Rawcus strutted along his rod towards the window. "Giss a kiss, love!" he blurted at the copper, poking his pointy pink tongue.

"What the fuck?" said the startled copper.

"He's just being friendly," said Joe. "You can always say, no."

The copper thrust his gun at Joe. "Get out!"

Rawcus squawked. "This won't end well, love! This won't end well, love!"

The copper shook his head at Rawcus. "Where does he get that crap from?"

Joe climbed out of the Firefly. "He grew up in a pub and he remembers stuff. He's got big ears."

The lawman snorted dismissively. "You feather-brains shoulda fucked off when you had the chance."

Rawcus had an ear cocked to the conversation. Joe sighed and stepped towards the front of the Firefly.

"Hey!" yelled the copper, who followed Joe. "Did I say you could move?"

Joe acted deaf, which was partly true. He took a few more steps and leaned back against the engine grill. The copper circled in front of him and aimed at Joe's chest with a double-handed grip.

Joe poked the tip of a little finger into his dodgy ear, pulled it out, and pretended to examine it for wax, all the while focussing his eyes beyond his fingertip onto the shrub inside which he hoped Lennie was still crouched.

"Turn around and face the van," the copper ordered, keeping his pistol in one hand while he reached with the other for the cuffs on his belt.

Joe noticed a glistening object spinning towards them from the forest.

The steel head of Lennie's tomahawk clipped the wrist of the copper's gun-toting hand. *Ka-thack!* The copper's wild shot echoed. The tomahawk crash-landed with a puff of dust and spun to a stop up the track. The copper squealed. Despite his torn flesh and chipped bone, the lawman held his pistol and used his good hand to lift his damaged appendage so he could renew his aim at Joe, who was sprinting at him.

Joe's snap-kick landed inside the copper's groin, connecting with more shinbone than foot, but it compressed his target's baby-makers with sufficient effect. Joe's follow-through lifted the man off the ground as he blasted another round that smashed through Lennie's bush.

The lawman doubled over, groaning. Joe grabbed him by his hacked wrist and squeezed; he figured he'd touched the nerve he was after when the copper yelped and dropped the gun, whereupon Joe head-locked him in the crook of an arm that covered much of the copper's jaw as well as neck.

Lennie emerged from the bush, checking himself for unwanted holes, and deciding there were none, he quickstepped towards the fallen pistol. He bent to pick it up.

An alien voice barked at Lennie from behind: "Don't fuckin' touch it!"

Lennie and Joe turned as one to face the speaker. Their eyes popped wide. A young white man, naked except for a pair of grey socks, was pointing his stiff penis to the sky and a pistol at them. He swung the barrel from side-to-side like he wasn't sure who to shoot first.

The gunslinger growled, "You ugly pricks have really stuffed up my day."

Lennie, sensing the nude nutter had been taking seriously good drugs, and possibly Viagra, given the proud state of his reproductive organ, said, "*That* is a very small cock you have."

The gunslinger's face took on a puzzled look and he stared down as if to see if this assertion had any foundation in fact.

"It looks like a red bantam," said Joe as dispassionately as a farmer judging livestock. "Not much to see when they're all plucked like that."

"Buck-buck, bu-gurk," chortled Lennie.

The gunslinger's eyes darted in various directions as if he was seeing and hearing things that weren't really there.

"Don't sweat, mate," called Lennie. "Best thing to do is hope you're hallucinating this entire scene."

The naked gunslinger started shaking.

Joe had a think: while Lennie's line of attack had clearly unbalanced the man, Joe was unsure whether this might cause him to take a pot shot at Lennie – or at Joe, despite his makeshift copper-shield – in an attempt to sift ghost from man, dream from reality. But then a vision began appearing before Joe, and he relaxed a little.

Behind the gunslinger, a naked young woman was stepping as daintily as a ballerina. Her skin was as white as the inside of a new teacup, her shoulder-length hair a dark mess, and her eyes were black behind the tangled tresses that straddled her ghostly face. By her right leg, she was swinging Lennie's tomahawk, which in her hand appeared more like an axe. She was wearing a single red sandal. Joe tightened his arm-lock on the copper's throat, restricting his captive's vocal range to a gurgle and making his eyeballs almost pop from his head. The girl closed in.

Using both her hands, she took a backswing, and with an emphasis on accuracy over ferocity, she drove the hawk's blade into the gunslinger's skull.

"Shoulda. Fucked off!" cried Rawcus, who had climbed through the van's window and was eyeing proceedings from atop the Firefly's wing mirror.

• • • •

WE HOPE YOU ENJOYED the opening to *Kangaroo Court*.

Learn more, find more books, or join the Mark Furness Readers Club to get free books by visiting his website: www.markfurnesswriter.com[1]

• • • •

OTHER BOOKS BY MARK Furness:

Under Eden, an international crime trilogy: #1 *The Ebola Conspiracy; #2 Freefall; #3 Red Box*. The Gar Hart journalist thrillers.

• • • •

SHORT STORIES:

The Trespasser: A View to Die For.

Drink with a Stranger: Journey to the Bizarre in Delhi, India.

Hugo's Awakening: A Mind-bending Road Trip to the Australian Outback.